A NEW BEGINNING

Goodwin the groom was ambling across the courtyard. It was about time to check up on that young tearaway, Vicky Denning. He couldn't help liking her, anyone who loved horses like she did couldn't be all bad.

He approached the main stable entrance and suddenly, a black flash and a ripple of muscle exploded past him. Goodwin leapt to one side, narrowly avoiding being bowled over by the four-legged charger.

"You fool," he yelled. Squinting in after the culprit, he could see the black horse already disappearing into the distance. But even at that range, there was no mistaking the rider: young Vicky Denning – and she wasn't riding sidesaddle.

Coming soon from Knight Books:

The New Adventures of Black Beauty:
FRESH HORIZONS

The New Adventures of Black Beauty

Executive Producer	Tom Parkinson
Producer	Murray Newey
Associate Producer	Brian Walden
Creative Consultant	Anthony S. Gruner
Original Script devised by	Ken Catran
Directors	John Crome, Katherine Millar, Mike Smith
Starring	Amber McWilliams as Vicky Stacy Dorning as Jenny Bill Lucas as Dr Gordon Gedeon Burkhard as Manfred

The New Adventures of Black Beauty is an Isambard
Production in association with Fremantle International
and London Weekend Television

The New Adventures of
Black Beauty

A NEW BEGINNING

Jonathan Dowling

KNIGHT BOOKS
·**Hodder and Stoughton**

First published in Great Britain in 1990 by Knight Books

The characters and situations in this book are entirely imaginary and bear no relation to any real person or actual happenings.

Printed and bound in Great Britain for Hodder and Stoughton Paperbacks, a division of Hodder and Stoughton Ltd., Mill Road, Dunton Green, Sevenoaks, Kent TN13 2YA. (Editorial Office: 47 Bedford Square, London WC1B 3DP) by Cox & Wyman Ltd., Reading, Berks.
Photoset by Chippendale Type Ltd., Otley, West Yorkshire.

British Library C.I.P.

A Catalogue record for this book is available from the British Library

ISBN 0 340 54576 3

1

It wouldn't be long now. Vicky could tell. Even with her eyes closed, or more especially with her eyes closed, she knew exactly where she was. She could time, almost to the second, when the driver would flick his whip and wheel the trap around to begin that long, sweeping arc which marked the entrance to Fordham Manor.

Those sounds coming from her grandfather's horse and trap gave the game away. The large iron-rimmed wheels and horse's hooves, which had been biting silently into soft ground, now emitted the harsh ringing noise of metal on gravel.

They had already ridden over a gentle rise – the old brick bridge which Vicky loved. She had tried but couldn't resist a peep. Quickly her eyes shut again and she blocked their position from her mind, not wanting to spoil the game.

Crack! There it was. She sensed the horse shift slightly and felt the gentle change of direction brought about so easily by her driver. The brisk autumn air made her skin glow and the sun, when it burst through the high cloud, simply made things perfect.

What a day to return!

Eight . . . seven . . . six . . . five. Vicky began her countdown, developed and refined on every visit.

There was the wind from the nearby oaks which acted as another of her markers. Now, if she had allowed just the right amount of time for the speed of her carriage, it should only be a matter of seconds.

Three . . . two . . . one . . . open.

And there it was. This time she had judged it perfectly.

Fordham Manor. That first full sight always gave Vicky a thrill. It was never the same catching early glimpses over the treetops or through the heavy thickets that lined her way. This way was best. To open your eyes and see the manor standing in front of you, huge and so magnificent – well, no one in New Zealand would ever believe it.

'Vicky.' Lord Fordham marched down the wide front steps, arms outstretched, to greet her. 'You're late. I was beginning to get worried.'

'It's all right, grandfather. I couldn't leave school as early as I'd have liked. Had to take a later train.'

'I was about to send Barret out looking for you.'

'He wouldn't have found me.'

Vicky couldn't imagine anything worse. Having to ride five miles from the railway station to her grandfather's with that coarse unfriendly man, who was always trying to turn her against her other friends on the estate.

Vicky had had her troubles adjusting to English schools but, she thought, her time at this latest one had been well spent in one regard at least. She had discovered a word that described Barret down to a tee. Obsequious. Exactly. He spent half his life fawning and being so smarmy to her grandfather it was almost laughable. The rest of the time, he was ill-tempered and surly to everyone else.

'Come along,' Lord Fordham said, marching her into the house. 'You've just enough time to change. You can fit in an hour's hard ride before supper.'

Normally, nothing would have pleased Vicky more. Riding was her passion, and her grandfather knew it. And he was only trying to be nice.

But it had been an exhausting day – she hadn't really missed her train, the headmistress had kept her back for 'insolence'. In the two years Vicky had spent in England, she had come to learn that insolence was when a young woman spoke her mind. Her elders – teachers especially – weren't used to that at all. They liked it even less coming from a 'little colonial', as they so disdainfully described anyone coming from Australia or New Zealand.

Miss Pratchett had made her scrub the floors in the dormitory. It took her three hours of strenuous effort. When she had finished, her back hurt, her neck ached and she could feel every muscle in her right arm from wrist to shoulder. And every one of them hurt like mad.

'I don't think we need to say a word about this to your grandfather,' Miss Pratchett had said in a stern tone of warning. 'Lord Fordham is a busy man and I think we can safely say you've learnt your lesson . . . '

Vicky had suppressed a desire to tell Miss Pratchett exactly *what* lesson she'd learned. That it didn't pay to talk back to people whose only function in life was to inflict misery on others. But Vicky's body cried out for rest, and even a bumpy train journey and the ride to Fordham Manor would seem like luxury after such hard work.

Of course, she couldn't tell Lord Fordham any of this. He had such hopes for her and, more than anything else, he wanted her to be happy – further bad news from school would weigh heavily upon him.

'I'd love a ride, grandfather, but I have to unpack first,' Vicky said as tactfully as she could.

'Mary will do all that.'

Vicky had forgotten about all the servants. It took a while to get used to having everything done for you again after the rigours of boarding school.

'Actually, I'm feeling a bit pooped after all that travelling.'

'Nonsense. A bit of exercise wipes away the cobwebs and gives one an appetite. Off you go.'

It was useless to argue. Vicky bounded up the stairs on aching legs, trying to look enthusiastic, then collapsed inside the room that Lord Fordham kept permanently for her.

It had been her mother's room. In fact it hadn't changed since her mother and father first left for New Zealand more than twelve years ago. They had made such a handsome couple, smiling happily, standing arm-in-arm on the dockside, waiting to board their ship.

Vicky looked at them, frozen in a happier time, in the silver-framed photograph which took pride of place on her dresser.

It still felt odd, seeing them as Sarah and Nigel Denning, prior to her own somewhat eventful arrival on the scene. Her mother had told her the story so often that now it seemed almost like a fairytale – like one of those special stories imprinted in your subconscious, that gives you goosebumps of pleasure each time you hear it, no matter how old you become.

'We were three days out from Sydney, in the midst of the worst storm we'd encountered in all our months at sea. Daddy was the doctor, so he was there too, and we waited and waited, but you took your time. You're never one to be rushed, a very strongwilled child – we both said that.

'Then suddenly, there you were. An adorable bundle of energy. Compared with you, even that nasty old storm knew it had met its match, because it stopped the very moment you arrived. Your father and I knew then we had a very, very special girl on our hands.'

Then always the story would finish with a warm cuddle and gentle kiss, before her mother turned out the lights and quietly left Vicky alone to sleep.

Vicky smiled sadly at the memory. It was two years since her mother's death and, despite what everybody kept telling her, the agony and loneliness didn't seem any more distant.

But it had changed. It was hard to explain. The hurting didn't stop, but the periods in between Vicky's sad times had grown a little longer.

Slowly, she replaced the precious photograph and sat on the bed, still looking at it – not wanting to break the gaze or her link with the past. It seemed silly, she knew, but it was as though if she waited there long enough or wished for it hard enough, she just might conjure her mother back to life.

Two years wasn't that long ago. The family had been content, or so it had seemed to Vicky, on their small New Zealand farm. Daddy's medical practice was growing as more and more people flocked to the colonies. Then, she could remember, things got much busier for him. He was out most of the day and much of the night, and when he got back he was often too tired to play with her as he had done in the past.

Everyone seemed worried, they were talking about an epidemic.

A disease, diphtheria, had a firm grip on the country. People were dying in their thousands. Then, suddenly, Daddy didn't go out much any more. He stayed with Mother in their room. One day he emerged, and it was done. He couldn't look her in the face, but Vicky knew what had happened. She ran in to see her mother lying, calm and porcelain white, in her bed where earlier she had been so feverish.

Vicky had known then, through her tears, that their lives would never be the same again. With her father, she had tried to adjust but neither of them could do anything to lift the pall of gloom which had descended.

Barely two months after Sarah Denning died, Vicky and her father were sailing home to England, the Old Country. It was 1901 – the beginning of a new century and the end of an era. The whole British Empire was in mourning, following the death of Queen Victoria.

And the world was changing. Beneath the formal grief, an air of excitement and fresh expectation was clearly discernible. But that excitement completely eluded Vicky and Nigel Denning. Both felt cut off and alone, even once they had arrived safely back on English soil.

Vicky stirred on the bed in her mother's old room. Her father, she now decided, had emerged from their self-imposed shell more quickly and easily than she. Things had changed quickly, all right, even in the past few months. There was still a great deal in her life for her to work out.

2

Vicky's train of thought was broken by echoing footsteps along the corridor. They stopped outside her room, and she turned as the door to her bedroom opened.

Mary's face peeped around the corner.

'Welcome home, luv. Let me look at you. Aren't you a sight for sore eyes, then? Haven't they been feeding you at that 'orrible place? Don't you worry. I'll have cook whip you up summ't that'll put the flesh back on those bones.'

Vicky tried to answer, but once Mary got going there was little one could do but let the verbal assault take its course.

'I'll say one thing, though. You've grown. Even with 'em not feeding you proper. Tell me . . . glad to be home? Course you are, who wouldn't be? We've all missed you, except Barret, of course – he has more of a run of things with you not here, if you know what I mean.'

Mary paused. 'Well c'mon luv, say something.'

After listening to Mary's non-stop prattle, Vicky was practically out of breath herself. But she smiled, 'Mary,' and launched herself into the old woman's arms.

'Ooh, it's good to have you back, Miss Victoria. I didn't get the chance to see you before you left – so soon after the wedding. I didn't like the thought of you leaving disturbed.'

'I wasn't disturbed, Mary. I had to go back straight away – the school wouldn't give me any more time off.'

This wasn't strictly true, but Vicky didn't want to go into details, even with Mary. Everyone just naturally assumed that Vicky would be upset when her father remarried, but she hadn't been really. She loved him and Jenny, his new wife, seemed a nice person.

What did worry her was that, since arriving in England, Vicky had been seeing less and less of her father. It wasn't his fault, she knew that. He had been studying for an advanced medical degree in London and Lord Fordham had insisted Vicky stay with him. Now, it seemed, whenever Daddy had free time Vicky was either in boarding school or on the continent with her grandfather. As father and daughter, their times together had been few and fleeting at that. When he told her he planned to remarry, well, it had been a shock. But they had talked it through, like they always did, and Vicky had accepted his right to a new life.

Again, Mary intruded on her thoughts.

'Now look, you leave the unpacking to me, right miss? And here's something Lord Fordham wanted me to dress you in special. For the riding.'

From behind the door, Mary whisked out two large boxes with a flourish and laid them on the bed. Inside was a smart new riding suit, complete with beautiful leather boots and crop.

It took Vicky's breath away.

'Direct from London, that is Miss Vicky,' Mary said, filling in every detail she could. 'Latest fashion.'

Vicky rushed past her, out on to the stairwell landing and leaned over the bannister.

'Grandfather, you shouldn't have.'

Her cry met with a deep chuckle from within Lord Fordham's study. He loved nothing better than giving his granddaughter 'special treats' and watching her reaction. And she never failed him –

nothing seemed to spoil her – every gift met with the same, excited response.

Vicky raced back to try it on.

'A riding habit. How does he always know exactly what I want?'

'Grandfathers just know, that's all,' came Mary's wise reply. 'That's their job. And Lord Fordham, I reckon he knows it as well or better'n most. Here, let me help you on with it – no need to rush with these things, you'll do yourself a mischief.'

'It's a little tight, I think,' Vicky puffed, squeezing into her new outfit. 'We might have to do some alterations.'

'I don't think so, you know. These things are meant to be tight – it complements a woman's figure.' Mary cackled with laughter at Vicky's obvious embarrassment.

'Don't mind me, you look a picture. Now, off you go. Show your grandfather how much you've grown.'

Vicky stood at the top of the stairs. The riding habit certainly was tight. She moved forward. Drat! It was hard enough negotiating these stairs; how on earth could she straddle a horse properly like this?

Fashion was all very well, thought Vicky, but it could be very frustrating. What was the point of looking nice if it stopped you doing the things you wanted?

Vicky sighed. She must try to curb her tongue – she couldn't disappoint Lord Fordham after all he'd done.

'That's right. That's it. Make sure you get the saddle on tight.'

Lord Fordham was standing, feet astride, in front of the stables, supervising the groom.

'I won't have anything happening to her! You'll be the first one I'll blame if anything . . . why, Vicky!'

He'd heard her coming. Well, anyone would have. You can't even *walk* quietly in this. Vicky was starting to get cross.

'Grandfather. Thank you for everything. You know that. But I can't ride in this. Look at it.'

Vicky spread the skirt as wide as it could go which wasn't very far.

'Yes you can. It's made for riding. All the young ladies wear them and so shall you.'

Lord Fordham indicated to the mare being saddled up behind him. Vicky followed his gesture and stared in disbelief. For a moment she was utterly speechless. Her grandfather chuckled happily, mistakenly thinking she was gazing spellbound at the horse.

'Do you like her?'

'It's a sidesaddle!' Vicky couldn't hold back her disgust even if she wanted to. 'You know what I think about sissy sidesaddle riding.'

'Nothing better for a young lady's constitution,' Lord Fordham replied.

'But I've never ridden like that.'

Her protests were met with an indulgent smile. 'You're not in the colonies now, Victoria. This is how a young lady rides. Hop up, you'll be riding the hounds in no time.'

'I'll be falling off in no time, too.'

The groom was there waiting, hands crossed, to help her up. There was nothing else for it. Vicky accepted his offer, put her nice new boot in his hands and attempted to mount the mare. Really, this was too silly. It wasn't so hard getting there, but once the groom moved away, Vicky felt like a proper fool – perched on the edge of a cliff, knowing she was going to fall.

And what was worse, she had an audience to laugh at her when she succumbed to the inevitable. Grandfather, the groom and a couple of stablehands – they were all there watching. So what? She was as good a rider as any of them, probably better, and they knew it. How happy would they be if someone dumped them on a saddle as absurd and illogical as this?

The horse moved slightly and off Vicky slid. She sat on the cobblestones, steaming, waiting for the raucous laughter she was sure would follow. But there was only silence. No one said a word, their attention had turned elsewhere. From the side of the house a familiar voice rang out.

'Now that's something I never expected to see. Vicky Denning riding sidesaddle – and not too well at that.'

'Father!' Vicky was up and running before the words were out of Nigel Denning's mouth. 'When did you get back?'

'Today, of course. Didn't you get my telegram?'

Vicky disentangled herself from their embrace and looked at him confused. She was just about to say no, when Lord Fordham interrupted.

'I did.' There was a long silence, as both Nigel and Vicky looked at him, silently asking the obvious question – why hadn't he told his granddaughter?

'I must have got the date wrong.'

The tone in his voice had gone quite flat, and the look which passed between the two men betrayed a tension, even enmity, that wasn't lost on those present – even Vicky felt it, torn as she was between them both.

'Lucky I got here when I did then,' Nigel said, breaking the ice and giving his daughter another warm hug. But he had half an eye on Lord Fordham as he told her, 'You'd have been over the hills and far away in another few minutes . . .'

'I wouldn't have got very far wearing this horrible thing,' Vicky laughed.

Even before she'd said it, she wished she hadn't. As the words came out, she saw her grandfather flinch at the way she had ridiculed his gift.

Then, immediately she realised the effect of her words, her attitude changed to one of defiance. *It's hardly my fault, is it?* she thought. If grandfather hadn't been so set on me riding in that old-fashioned way, this would never have happened.

It was a bad characteristic, Vicky's stubborn streak, inherited from equally headstrong parents. When she felt she was right, she wouldn't bend to anybody. In the colonies, such behaviour was tolerated to a greater degree than in more rigid British society. It had got her into a few scrapes in New Zealand, but it had caused no end of problems at the English private schools she'd attended.

Vicky was intelligent enough to realise all this, but it didn't help. No matter how much she wanted to, she couldn't apologise to her grandfather.

Instead she avoided his gaze, staring down at the ground and her lovely new boots – part of Lord Fordham's present. And that made her feel even worse.

Lord Fordham watched her reaction carefully, waiting for some kind of apology. He couldn't understand Vicky sometimes, and try as he might he never would. All he saw was an ungrateful girl who was spiting him in front of his former son-in-law (didn't he have enough trouble with him as it was?) and, what was even worse, his servants.

He waited, then sighed, before speaking again. 'You've got half-an-hour to try and make those "horrible" clothes work for you, not against you. Your father and I have some business to discuss.'

'Yes.' Nigel Denning was already walking away from her into the house. Vicky stared after him. Obviously there were more important things than talking to his own daughter, whom he hadn't seen since his wedding day three months before.

Right, she thought. If that's the way they want it, I *will* ride off. See if I care. She turned away and spied, a short distance off from her own mare, her father's horse, a magnificent old black stallion.

'Can I ride this horse, father? He's a real beauty.'

By the time Nigel Denning heard her and turned around, Vicky was beside the stallion, stroking its nose and whispering to it quietly.

'He is a beauty,' Nigel called back. 'That's Black Beauty. Jenny's horse. If you want to ride him I'm afraid you'll have to ask her.'

The two men disappeared inside. Vicky moved over to her mare and attempted to mount the awkward-shaped saddle, then gave up in disgust. She dismissed the groom, who led the horse away quietly, and then turned her attention to Black Beauty.

'If no one else wants to talk to me, I think I'll talk to you. I know, what about a nice rubdown in Lord Fordham's stables and a good feed of oats? Does that sound good?'

Vicky took Beauty's reins and followed the groom over the courtyard cobblestones to the soft straw-covered earth of the stables.

Goodwin, the head groom, eyed the new arrival suspiciously.

'You shouldn't be treating this horse here without his lordship's permission,' he chided her.

'My father rode him here. He needs a rubdown.' Vicky could sense a confrontation about to occur.

'Aye, I know the horse. He's a fine animal. Be that as it may, he belongs to Jenny Gordon, and his lordship don't hold with her and her ways.'

'She's Jenny Denning, now. That's my step-mother you're talking about,' Vicky snapped back. There, that got him. She didn't think she'd ever be defending Jenny like this, but it wasn't fair talking about someone like that behind their back when they couldn't defend themselves.

Goodwin wandered off, muttering about women doing men's work and what things were coming to. Vicky knew he was referring to Jenny as much as he was about her own intrusion in the stables.

Jenny had caused quite a stir coming back to the area as a qualified vet. She had taken over the local practice from the retiring vet, but Lord Fordham wouldn't stand for a woman tending to his animals. He had barred her from his estate and taken on the services of a 'real vet' in the next village.

Silly men, thought Vicky, trapped today with yesterday's ideas. No matter, the confrontation had left her alone with Black Beauty. She collected a couple of brushes and began to give the horse a vigorous rubdown. Beauty snorted with pleasure.

'I'll bet you've never let anyone ride you side-saddle, have you Beauty?'

As Vicky worked, she knelt down, but the long dress hampered her movement. She exclaimed with annoyance, pulling it this way and that, but it didn't really help. Then her eyes came to rest on a range of tools hanging on a nearby wall. One of the items was a pair of very sharp steel shears.

'Beauty,' she whispered, 'I think we might be in luck.'

3

Vicky was wrong, of course, when she thought her father's business was more important than her. The subject Nigel Denning and Lord Fordham were discussing was Vicky herself.

Or more specifically, Vicky's future. The two men had quite different plans for her. Their differences had been apparent for over a year now, and the need to make a decision had become more pressing than ever. With only two weeks of school holidays available, Nigel had precious little time to get reacquainted with his daughter and convince her to return home with him to New Zealand.

'I don't think she's quite come to terms with having a stepmother,' Fordham was saying. 'It was all rather a . . . whirlwind courtship.'

Nigel smiled. 'That's Jenny. Swept me off my feet.'

'Mmmmm.' Lord Fordham frowned in disapproval. Sometimes he could say a lot by saying very little.

Nigel felt at a disadvantage as he was led through the grand old house. Its valuable heirlooms and lavish, though often quite impractical, design were all calculated to impress. This was Fordham's home turf – it had been in the family for centuries – but Nigel was determined not to be intimidated.

'She did meet Jenny before the wedding, sir.'

'Briefly.' Fordham's reply was practised and rapier swift, 'And she's seen precious little of you in the last two years. Oh, I know you've had your studies in London . . . '

This was getting out of hand. Fordham's voice was stopping just short of a sneer, but its intention was obvious. He was implying that Nigel had neglected his daughter and wasn't fit to keep her.

But it was no good overreacting. Lord Fordham had considerable power and would be prepared to use it. Nigel needed to keep his wits about him. He would have to chip away at the old man's defences and, at the same time, ignore the insults designed to make him lose control. He couldn't afford to appear hot-headed or unfit as a father.

He struggled to keep his voice under control. 'And every time I *am* free to see her, sir, she seems either to have been sent off to boarding school or is travelling overseas with you.'

'Victoria likes Italy. As did her mother.'

Nigel thought what he could not say. That any young girl likes being made a constant fuss of, and a rich doting grandfather can easily make every day seem like Christmas if that is his wish. That was not the real world, and it wasn't the way he wanted his daughter brought up.

But that line of argument was useless. For at that moment Lord Fordham wasn't in the real world either – he was far away, lost in thought. Nigel followed his gaze to a picture of Sarah and Vicky, taken on the steps of their New Zealand homestead seven years before.

Fordham sighed. 'They were so very alike.'

Tears welled in his eyes. He lingered another moment on the photograph then turned back to Nigel, indicating with a regal nod of his head that their conversation could now resume.

Nigel hesitated. Lord Fordham was a formidable adversary. As a negotiator his feats for the British Government were legendary, and to retain his granddaughter he would use every means at his disposal. Nor was he above using emotional black-mail to achieve his purpose. Nigel had no doubt that Fordham's tears were real, but he was equally certain that Fordham had chosen that moment for a purpose. Well, he wouldn't be made to feel sorry for the old man – this was too important.

'You always wanted what was best for Sarah. I want what is best for my daughter,' Nigel began carefully.

'I *know* what is best for her.' Lord Fordham's reply was as curt as his next statement was cutting. 'Just as I knew what was best for Sarah.'

'As you'll recall, sir, Sarah made the decision to emigrate with me over exactly the same objections raised by you.'

'And perhaps if she hadn't . . . ' Fordham's voice trailed off, leaving the rest of his thoughts to hand in mid-air.

'She was my wife,' Nigel said quietly. 'You're not the only one who suffered.'

'But now you have another wife – another life.'

'Not one removed from my own daughter, I should hope.'

'Victoria is my sole heir. She will be very wealthy . . . she must understand her place in society. That's what her mother would have wished.'

'But Vicky has been used to a free and inde-pendent life. Those things are just as important – more important to her than money or her "place in society" as you put it.'

Nigel's retort drew a cold look from the elder man. 'If by freedom, you mean wild spirits and general misbehaviour, then yes, clearly she had become far too used to it. That's why she had to be taken out of her first school, and it's a compelling reason why she should stay here with me now.'

Fordham was beginning to warm to his subject.

'I have very quietly brought her to heel. She's high-spirited, I'll grant you, and I don't want to change that. But she's learning and growing into quite the young lady. Victoria should grow up here in her mother's house. Not on some small-holding on the edge of nowhere. Man, what are her chances there?'

'She'll make her own. As did Sarah.'

'Your colonial farm, moreover, is in need of capital development.'

'Which you offered, sir.'

'Yes, I did. Subject to an agreement.'

So that was it, thought Nigel. Fordham's playing his last card. He'd made such a display of insisting Vicky both wanted and deserved to stay in England. But his final word betrayed his insecurity. It was clear he wasn't at all sure that Vicky wanted to stay with him, and he would do whatever was necessary to persuade her father to return to New Zealand without her.

But he'd seriously misjudged the kind of man Nigel Denning was.

'Sir, you are the trustee of Vicky's inheritance. You can make the decision to help us or hurt us, however you see fit. But remember, as a trustee you should have Vicky's best interests at heart. That money should be used to help the girl, not hinder her progress and it is not to be held up as some kind of ransom demand to keep her away from her father.'

Nigel's voice rose heatedly as he spoke. He knew he was overstepping the mark but he didn't care. He didn't care who Lord Fordham was, no one was going to treat him like this. He couldn't trade his daughter for money. If they had to return to New Zealand penniless and start from scratch, so be it.

Lord Fordham, meanwhile, had listened to this tirade from the younger man with no outward sign of emotion. He brought both index fingers to his lips, forming a 'church steeple', and tucked his thumbs under his chin, considering Nigel's outburst. He said nothing. The two men sat in silence for several minutes, before Nigel spoke again.

'Vicky will be happier at home.'

At this Fordham bristled. 'This is her home.' He paused. 'I'm curious, Nigel. Have you ever asked her if she wants to return to New Zealand?'

'With respect, sir, have you?'

Lord Fordham could not reply. He hadn't asked Vicky, because deep down he feared her answer. He lifted himself out of his ornate leather chair and rang a small crystal bell on the mantelpiece.

Seconds later, Finlayson the butler, entered the room. Lord Fordham turned to Nigel.

'Would you care for some tea?'

Their meeting was over. Nothing had been resolved.

4

Goodwin the groom was ambling across the inner
courtyard. It was about time to check up on that
young tearaway. She was a funny girl, that Vicky,
he thought, but he couldn't help secretly liking her.
After all, anyone who loved horses like she did
couldn't be all bad. And he had to admit, she was as
good with horses as any of his lads at the stables.

He approached the main stable entrance – two
heavy oak doors which were standing wide open.
He'd have words with the stablehands about that.
Those doors were supposed to remain shut.

Suddenly, a black flash and a ripple of muscles
exploded past him. Goodwin leapt to one side,
narrowly avoiding being bowled over by the four-
legged charger.

'You fool,' he yelled after it, squinting into
the sun to see who the culprit was.

The black horse was already disappearing into the
distance. Its rider turned and waved happily back at
him. Even at that range there was no mistaking who
it was. Young Vicky Denning. Goodwin couldn't
be sure, but she didn't look as if she was riding
sidesaddle, the way a lady should.

What absolute, total relief! This was more like it,
Vicky thought. This, in fact, was the only way to
ride. Her once narrow skirt now flapped madly
about in the wind as horse and rider sped lightning-
fast across the fields. Vicky had cut it up the front
and back to allow her to straddle Black Beauty and

ride him the way he was meant to be ridden.

But the amazing thing about this horse was it didn't feel like riding at all. Most horses needed work, you had to concentrate on what you were doing and signal your intentions clearly to make sure it went where you wanted and when.

But Black Beauty was different. Special. Vicky had only to think of her next move and, by some miracle, Beauty seemed to sense exactly what it was. Subtle shifts on the saddle and a gentle flick of the wrist were all that he needed to dart off in another direction, or vary his speed. It was less like riding than being taken for an exhilarating ride.

And, despite Beauty's obvious age, he was still fast and strong. Jenny was so lucky to have such a magnificent stallion all to herself.

Vicky was thinking that Jenny was lucky in many respects. She had seen a lot more of Nigel Denning than Vicky had for a long time.

All these thoughts were whirling around Vicky's head as Black Beauty took her up and down the green rolling countryside, jumping fences with ease and guiding her through the odd maze of forests which dotted the Fordham estate.

In one such forest, Black Beauty began to slow, then came to a stop, whinnying softly. Vicky looked about, her eyes adjusting to the dim light. She heard a loud snap of metal close by; she could just make out the figure of a man bent over something on the ground about thirty feet away.

He glanced up as he drew closer. It was Barret. In front of him she could see the ugly iron jaws of a mantrap. At least half a dozen others were bulging out of a large sack he slung over his shoulder as he stood up and doffed his hat in greeting.

'Mind where you ride in these woods, Miss Victoria,' he said in his unpleasant, servile manner.

Vicky looked at him with distaste.

'What're you putting those things down for? They're cruel.'

'Because, ma'am, the head gamekeeper told me to. I'm only following orders.'

Barret was underkeeper on the estate, but he did pretty much what he wanted. Vicky knew that if, in fact, he had been told to lay these traps then he had probably suggested them in the first place. She fixed him with an icy stare.

'Aren't they illegal?'

'Lord Fordham's the law around here, Miss Victoria,' Barret replied with a mean smile. He took another trap out of his bag and placed it about twenty feet from the last, opening the spring-loaded jaws fast and covering it with the autumn leaves. Vicky looked on, sickened.

Barret looked up at her.

'Mind how you go on that horse,' he gloated. 'Sometimes even I can't remember where they all are.'

'I won't have any trouble, Barret. You're quite predictable really.'

Vicky gave Black Beauty a light touch with her heels and immediately they were off, kicking up a shower of leaves over Barret as they passed.

Barret stared after them, annoyed at the insult but not quick enough to dish out a parting rejoinder. He stomped away into the woods, unhappy with their encounter but satisfied he was getting his own back, laying the traps.

Black Beauty had decided to take the lakeside path. That was fine by Vicky, it was one of her favourite places – quiet and quite unspoiled. Looking ahead, she smiled and reined in, dismounting quietly.

She tied Beauty to the tree, stroking his nose and

whispering at him to keep silent. Then she crept stealthily forward towards the lake edge.

Ah, she was right. There he was. A short distance in front of her, partly hidden by some bushes, a man was lying full-length on the ground with an arm in the water.

Vicky got up as close as she dared, a delighted smile on her face. She assumed a mock frown and shouted out in the deepest voice she could muster:

'Caught you this time, Craddon!'

The man reacted as if he had been struck, leaping almost straight up into the air and whirling around to meet him opponent.

'What! I . . .'

He was breathing heavily, shocked and scared. Vicky nearly collapsed with laughter.

'Here, Miss Vicky, don't scare a man like that.'

He put his wet hand over his heart, still recovering from his scare. It took some effort, but Vicky finally stopped laughing and again looked serious.

'Seth, were you after my grandfather's trout again?'

'No. No. Of course not. I was . . . ah . . . washing my hands. I don't like the taste of trout no more.'

Vicky smiled knowingly and glanced at Seth's rumpled old jacket on the ground. A trout's head stuck out of one of the pockets.

'Are you taking that one home as a pet?'

Seth followed her gaze and could see the game was up. His shoulders slumped, discouraged, and he looked back at Vicky, shamefaced. It was hard for him to say the words that followed.

'I have to feed me kids, and work's hard to find these days.'

Vicky could see he wasn't lying. She had known Seth Craddon since she first arrived on the estate. He was a good, reliable man who had fallen on hard times. His wife had died six months ago, leaving him with four young ones to look after. If that wasn't bad enough, he'd lost his job as an apprentice blacksmith for spending too much time tending his sick wife. Now he was faced with hungry mouths to feed and no regular income.

Vicky hesitated. Seth had rejected her offers of help in the past. He was a proud man, but she considered that they were good friends. She felt around in her pocket and drew out a leather money pouch, offering him the contents.

This time it was Seth's turn to hesitate, but he accepted Vicky's offer.

'Thanks Missy,' he said with heartfelt gratitude. Vicky smiled.

'One of the underkeepers is setting traps by the lakeside. I think you know Barret, don't you?'

'We've had our run-ins,' Seth laughed. 'But he's not quite as quick as me. Thanks for the tip but don't worry, I'll keep well clear of him.'

'Somebody caught a deer the other night. Grandfather's furious . . . ' Vicky paused for a moment. 'It wasn't you by any chance?'

'Oh no, Missy. Too big for my pocket . . . ' He gave her one of his winning grins. Vicky could only smile – you could never tell with Seth, he was incorrigible.

'Go on, before Barret comes this way. And be careful.'

'Thanks Missy,' Seth touched his cap, grabbed his things and ducked off. He'd gone about a hundred yards, when he turned and yelled after her, 'Y'know, Missy, you're looking more like your mum every passing day . . . '

Vicky smiled and waved as Seth disappeared into the undergrowth. She walked over to Black Beauty, and led him down to the water to drink.

'You leave those trout alone, too, Beauty. I don't want grandfather after you as well.' The horse raised his head and looked at her quizzically. 'Don't worry, Beauty, it's a private joke.'

Suddenly, a gunshot sounded down the lake. A flock of birds flew up, squawking loudly. Black Beauty whinnied in alarm. Vicky listened as the sound died away in small, flat echoes. Then, determined, she mounted Beauty and raced off down the path.

It was only a matter of seconds before she was back where she had met Barret. Across to her left, she could see Seth Craddon running away. Vicky frowned, concerned, then swung around on hearing a cry from the lakeside.

There was Barret, kneeling on the ground, obviously in pain. His left hand was clutched tight around his right shoulder, blood trickling between his fingers.

'Please Ma'am, get some help. I've been shot.'

'Shot?' Vicky didn't like the sound of this. 'How?'

'Craddon. It were Seth Craddon. Please . . . get some help!'

Nigel Denning and Lord Fordham emerged from inside the manor and stood facing each other somewhat awkwardly on the massive front steps.

Lord Fordham extended his hand to Nigel in a rare gesture of friendship. Maybe he thinks he's won, thought Nigel, as they shook hands. I hope he's prepared for round two . . .

Fordham turned and stared expansively out over his lush, well-tended grounds. It made him feel most agreeable, and he momentarily forgot about their previous disagreement.

'I think once you spend a bit more time with Vicky, you'll change your mind about things, Nigel,' he said, using the young man's name for the first time. 'A first-rate school and solid environment . . . she's changing, and so is her attitude towards living here.'

Nigel was about to reply, but the sound of clattering hooves of an approaching horse distracted him. Fordham, however, wasn't going to let anything stop him once he got started.

'You saw for yourself, she's looking the very picture of a young English . . . gentlewoman.'

As the words fell from his lips, he made out the hatless, slit-skirted figure of his granddaughter approaching them at full gallop.

'I see what you mean,' Nigel said with a wry smile. Then he realised just which horse she was riding, and added, 'An English gentlewoman, moreover, who disobeys her father's instructions.'

'What's that?'

'She's riding Black Beauty.'

'Oh . . . ah . . . yes,' Fordham was off balance, quite shocked at the brazenness of Vicky's improvised riding suit.

Both men braced themselves, each mentally preparing the speech they would unleash on the young offender. Vicky came to a halt and leapt down from Black Beauty, breathless.

'Grandfather, Barret's been shot!'

All worries about Vicky's behaviour vanished. Nigel Denning immediately became the concerned doctor.

'How is he?'

'I don't think it's that bad. It's in his shoulder, but he's lost a lot of blood.'

Nigel sprinted down the manor steps, mounted Black Beauty and wheeled him about.

'You don't know where he is,' Fordham shouted.

'Don't worry. Beauty will take me there. Round

up some help and have them follow Vicky . . . '

'Goodwin! Browning! Pearson!' Lord Fordham roared. From various parts of the manor, men sprang to life, running at their master's call. And Fordham directed them with the seasoned air of someone born to give orders.

With Barret safely retrieved and Nigel's expert medical attention, the underkeeper was never in any serious danger.

'It'll be stiff for a day or two,' Nigel announced. 'I'll dress it again tomorrow.'

'Thank you doctor,' Barret turned to Lord Fordham, 'I saw him, m'Lord, with the fish. I started to follow but he whipped out his gun and took a shot. It was plain murder.'

Just then, Seth Craddon appeared struggling before them, forcibly held by Goodwin and another groom.

'And that's what you'll be charged with, Craddon,' Lord Fordham said grimly. 'Attempted murder.'

'The shot came from near you, Mr Barret,' Seth protested bitterly. 'I never saw no gun. I never even had one.'

Vicky couldn't hold back any longer. 'Grandfather, I met Seth earlier. He didn't have a gun.'

'I saw him with it, m'Lord.' Barret was insistent.

'No!' Craddon and Vicky cried in dismay.

'Summon the constable,' barked Fordham. Goodwin scampered off to do his bidding.

'But grandfather, he didn't . . . '

'You will keep out of this, Vicky. It is none of your concern.'

Craddon stared despairingly after her as he was hustled away, out of sight. Vicky started to run after him but Nigel intervened, holding her back. 'Vicky . . . '

He faced her square on, serious. 'Leave it alone.

31

Now, remember, we're taking tea this afternoon with Jenny.' He glanced over her tattered skirt. 'A change of clothes might be in order.'

Vicky stared in the direction Seth had been taken. 'Do I have to?'

'Yes, Victoria; you do.' Vicky hesitated a moment, then reluctantly allowed her father to lead her back towards the house.

Lord Fordham, overhearing their exchange, smiled quietly. Vicky's reaction to a visit with Jenny was more than he could have hoped for.

Goodwin led Black Beauty out of the stables, clucking his tongue gently at him. The head groom may have been a bit of a terror with people, but he knew and loved his horses. Even though he wouldn't admit it to Vicky, this black stallion was extraordinary – almost a freak – a thoroughbred to be sure, but a rare beast, even for one of remarkable pedigree.

And . . . Goodwin couldn't quite put his finger on it, he couldn't find the right words. Black Beauty 'looked intelligent', that was all. He reacted as though he understood what you were thinking. It was a bit eerie, thought Goodwin, who wasn't really given to thinking about such things.

He harnessed Beauty to Fordham's trap and waited for Nigel and Vicky. When they came out, Goodwin noted she had changed. 'Sunday best,' he said in approval.

Vicky caught what he'd said and registered a shy smile.

Her father took the reins, and they set off. To be honest, Vicky wasn't really looking forward to this, and she was still thinking about poor old Seth. Her father, though, was intent upon getting the two women in his life happily together.

'Vicky, I would like you to spend as much time

with Jenny as possible . . . ' He looked at her to check her reaction. She wasn't even listening. 'Vicky?'

'I can't believe it. Grandfather wouldn't even talk to me.'

'Weren't you listening to me?'

Vicky turned to her father, pleading. 'Take me to the lakeside. Please father. Let me show you where it happened.'

'Vicky,' Nigel sighed, and gave up for the moment. He knew there wouldn't be any rest until his daughter had at least attempted to persuade him of Seth's innocence. He would like to believe her – he had known Seth for a long time, but the evidence did seem to be against him.

They parked along the lakeside path and dismounted, Vicky leading the way.

'Seth was down the path with me. He couldn't have come this far in such a short time.'

Nigel followed cautiously. 'You be careful of those traps.'

'Oh, I know where they are,' she replied confidently, her skirt whisking past two waiting open jaws, 'I just wish the animals did.'

'And the poachers,' Nigel smiled.

'Yes, and the poachers. I'm not lying to protect Seth, father. I don't think Barret actually saw who did it.'

Nigel tried to change the subject. 'Do you really like it here, Vicky?'

'I like Seth. I met him on my first day. He showed me badgers, foxes, an otter. All the animals I'd never seen before. Now they've arrested him – it's not fair.'

'Your grandfather is bound by his position, Vicky. Oh yes, he gives you everything you want, but he's still Lord Fordham, and he still believes in his word being law. He won't brook any argument, even from you.'

'It's not fair. It wouldn't be allowed in New Zealand,' Vicky said again with feeling. She moved off again but Nigel stopped her. He cleared some leaves away with his foot to reveal, where she was going to tread, the jaws of a mantrap. Vicky looked down, stunned, then picked up a stick and thrust it into the trap. 'These things wouldn't be allowed, either.'

'That's one of the reasons your mother and I chose to go there,' Nigel said, taking her arm. 'It's our home, and that's where you and Jenny and I belong. Of course, you can stay here with your grandfather if you wish. It's your decision.'

Vicky was silent for a moment, thinking. 'Grandfather's been very good to me,' she offered, 'and he is lonely.'

'But is that enough reason to stay?'

'I'm just a little confused, that's all.'

Nigel stroked her hair fondly. 'A bit wilful, a bit spoilt, a bit of a scamp . . . ' He gave her a great hug. 'And next time you want to ride Beauty, you ask Jenny, all right?'

'Yes, father. He's a beautiful horse, isn't he? Does Jenny ride a lot?'

'All the time.'

'Side-saddle?'

'Never!'

5

Jenny's father, Dr Gordon, was a distinguished-looking gentleman in his early sixties with a grey, neatly trimmed beard, a fondness for tweed and a good pipe of tobacco. He was standing, waiting for them, in front of his thatched cottage.

'Good afternoon, Dr Gordon,' Vicky said shyly.

'Delighted to see you again, Vicky,' he smiled, turning to greet Nigel. 'It's always a pleasure – she's much prettier than you, I'm afraid, Nigel.'

'Everyone says I take after my mother.' Oops, thought Vicky as she went inside, another slip of the tongue. She hadn't meant it to come out that way.

Dr Gordon glanced at Nigel, an amused twinkle in his eye. They both hoped it wasn't going to be too difficult.

They might have made it easier for Vicky and Jenny if the men had just relaxed and left them to it. In trying to tread as carefully as they could, their forced politeness simply made Vicky more uncomfortable and shy.

Halfway through the meal Jenny looked across at Nigel with an 'is this the right time' expression. Nigel gave a knowing nod of his head.

Jenny took a small parcel from her pocket and placed it in front of Vicky on the table.

'Victoria, I brought back a little memento of our honeymoon in Scotland for you.'

'Oh . . . thank you . . .' Vicky unwrapped a large brooch and held it up uncertainly.

'It's a brooch to pin a shawl with. An old Caledonian design.'

'Oh . . .'

'Perhaps I could call you Vicky?'

Vicky replied a little stiffly, 'I don't mind Victoria.' She replaced the brooch on the table and turned to her father. 'May I be excused?'

Before he could answer, she had already risen out of her chair. Nigel was about to say something, his face reddening in embarrassment at her behaviour in front of their hosts. But Jenny stepped in.

'Of course you can.'

Vicky promptly left the room. Nigel breathed in heavy exasperation. 'Old Fordham's turning her into a spoiled little brat.'

'She's nothing of the sort,' Jenny retorted, having seen the look which passed between the two men. 'Vicky's just confused, she's bewildered, and she's not a little frightened by everything that's happened to her over the past couple of years.

'It's all happened very quickly, and now she's having to come to terms with a new stepmother as well.'

'Hmmm,' mused Dr Gordon. 'Headstrong, a bit madcap . . . going her own way and getting into all sorts of misadventures and tomfoolery when she does.'

'That's Vicky,' laughed Nigel.

But Jenny knew what her father meant. She gave him an amused look. 'But you weren't talking about Vicky, were you, father? Well, you can talk among yourselves now – if you'll excuse me.'

She got up and left the table, following Vicky outside.

'Was she really as bad as all that?' Nigel asked Dr Gordon, curious at the possibility of another side to his new wife.

'Oh, worse,' Dr Gordon chuckled at the memory. 'Much worse.'

Vicky hadn't gone very far at all. In fact, she'd stopped directly outside the dining room door and had listened to the whole exchange. It felt a bit funny, being grateful to Jenny standing up for her like that. Then she remembered that she had stood up for Jenny when Goodwin made those remarks about her. They were even, she thought, hurrying off before Jenny caught her eavesdropping. Nevertheless, she couldn't help liking the new Mrs Denning just a little bit more than she had before.

When Jenny eventually found Vicky, she was standing stroking Black Beauty. His head was stretched forward towards her as she spoke to him, intelligently receiving her conversation.

'You'd rather ride Black Beauty than have some silly old brooch, wouldn't you?' Jenny said, drawing a startled reaction from Vicky who hadn't heard her come up.

'Oh! Yes . . . I mean, no . . . the brooch is lovely.'

'What do you think of Beauty?'

'Oh . . . he's magnificent.'

'He's been part of my life almost longer than I can remember. We belong to each other,' Jenny said with feeling. It made Vicky smile. This was a language she could talk – much easier than polite table manners.

'Is that why you became a vet?'

'Partly . . .'

'Why don't you come to grandfather's estate? There are a lot of animals there. You could also try and stop that awful trapping the gamekeepers do.'

'I'm afraid there are quite a few things your grandfather and I don't see eye to eye on,' Jenny paused. 'One of them is woman vets.'

'Yes. He can be a bit old-fashioned.' Vicky thought seriously for a few moments, then added, 'I wish I had a horse like Beauty.'

Both of them were stroking Beauty's mane. Their hands met and this time Vicky didn't pull away. She returned Jenny's smile, although still with some apprehension.

Black Beauty took the three Dennings back to Fordham Manor, over the old brick bridge by the lake.

'Look!' Vicky shouted.

Nigel and Jenny followed her outstretched finger. In the distance, about a dozen men were searching the lakeside and among the water reeds.

'I'll bet grandfather is looking for that gun.'

Nigel looked serious. 'Vicky, I have some important business to discuss with your grandfather tonight. Please don't upset him.'

Vicky appeared deflated, but she knew better than to argue with her father when he was in this mood. 'All right, father. But he is wrong about Seth.'

Jenny and Nigel exchanged anxious glances. Tonight would be difficult enough without Vicky further upsetting Lord Fordham.

But before the trap pulled up outside the manor, Vicky slipped off the back unnoticed. There was Barret, leaning up against a wall, gloating at her in his smug triumph over her and Seth.

Vicky confronted him, her little face screwed up in a fury which she now unleashed on this odious man.

'Barret, you know Seth didn't shoot you. Why are you lying?'

'I've said all I'm going to Miss. That man's a poacher – we're losing too much game.'

'And you haven't caught anyone, isn't that right?'

Vicky demanded angrily. 'That's why you're picking on Seth, isn't it?'

But the underkeeper didn't reply. He just stood, sullen and defiant.

'Who did shoot you?' Vicky was yelling now. But Nigel was quickly on the scene, and he pulled her away from the silent Barret.

'That's enough, Vicky.' He turned to face Barret himself, 'How's the arm?'

'Right enough, sir.'

'Good. Come along, Vicky.' He led the young girl away, back to the trap. Once they were out of Barret's earshot, he whispered to her. 'There's no use talking to him, Vicky. He'll close up like an oyster.'

'But there's something wrong about all this,' Vicky responded.

'Maybe so. But remember what I told you. Nothing on the subject of Seth Craddon over dinner.'

'No, father.'

'Or after dinner.'

'No, father.'

'Or before dinner.'

Vicky had to smile. He could always force a smile from her, no matter how concerned she was with things.

'Father, of course not,' she replied innocently. 'I don't know what you take me for.'

'A stubborn, self-willed, outspoken, independent young madam,' he answered affectionately.

'A little like Jenny, then?' Vicky was teasing him.

'How did you . . . ?' He laughed, exasperated, and took Vicky's hand in a tight clasp as they rejoined Jenny. Jenny smiled as she helped Vicky back up on the trap, but her smile faltered when she turned around – Lord Fordham was watching from an upstairs window.

Dinner was not a success. Lord Fordham had decided to keep it as formal as possible. He had three servants and Finlayson serving, with the best silver, and he'd insisted on formal dress for the men, complete with white bow ties. The manor had long been fitted with electricity, but tonight the room was lit by half a dozen magnificent silver candelabras strategically placed about the large room.

He had issued no formal instructions for the women; however Jenny and Vicky were under no illusions that they were expected to make a similar effort.

In fact, Vicky had to admit, Jenny looked quite beautiful in her cream silk dress. She wore her hair up and, with her dress cut just below the shoulder highlighting that stunning pearl necklace, she looked most sophisticated.

Lord Fordham sat aloof at the head of the table, seldom talking through most of the meal. Vicky chattered away happily, studiously avoiding the subject of Seth Craddon. But nothing seemed to lessen the tension that dominated the table.

When proceedings threatened to grind to a complete halt, Jenny made a final effort.

'Ah . . . perhaps Victoria might like to accompany me on my rounds tomorrow.'

Vicky looked up, intrigued at the prospect, but Fordham answered.

'Yours . . . is a very *novel* profession for a woman.' There was definitely a malicious tone to his voice.

Nigel cut in, 'Oh, there's quite a number of professional women in the colonies – isn't that so, Vicky?'

Vicky nodded her head. She didn't like being caught in the middle like this. Fordham ignored her anyway.

'I believe some occupations unsex a lady,' he stated, knowing full well this line was bound to draw a reaction. But Jenny was too clever to be irritated like this.

'Strange how they never seem to unsex a gentleman.'

Fordham gave her a long, hard look. She was sharp, he'd give her that. Let's see how she handled this one.

'That, young lady, is the order of society.'

But Jenny just smiled, refusing to be provoked. Fordham tried a different tack.

'Your work must necessitate long hours.'

'Yes it does.'

'And yours, Nigel.'

'Of course,' Nigel replied cautiously. Where was this leading?

'But what happens to Victoria? Who looks after her when both of you are out gallivanting around the colonies, consumed by your work?' Lord Fordham managed to make the word 'work' sound almost like a crime.

That was it. Jenny's mouth tightened, ready to deliver a damning retort. But Vicky stood up quickly.

'May I please go to bed? It's been a long day.'

Fordham softened. 'Of course, my dear.'

'Goodnight grandfather . . . father . . . ' Vicky moved around the table but on reaching Jenny she stopped, unsure how to address her new stepmother. Jenny solved the problem.

'Perhaps I could see Victoria to her room.'

Fordham stiffened – presumptious woman! But Jenny didn't wait for his approval. She guided Vicky out of the door. All Fordham could manage was a belated, 'As you wish.'

41

Left alone with him, Nigel could sense Fordham's hackles rising. Strong-willed women didn't sit well with such engrained Victorian values – Nigel wondered how men like Fordham ever accepted a queen as their absolute ruler.

There was a long silence. Lord Fordham prolonged it, deliberately taking his time over selecting a walnut from the sideboard and crushing it in his silver nutcracker.

Nigel wasn't going to be drawn into making the first move. He could bluff it out as long as anyone. He sat there, looking straight ahead, waiting.

Finally, Fordham addressed him. 'I will advance the finance you need, Nigel. I must insist, however, that Victoria remain here. After all, I am the trustee of her mother's legacy.'

Nigel breathed in deeply, before replying . . .

The two Denning women breathed a collective sigh of relief as soon as they were safely outside the dining room.

'I simply had to get out of there,' Jenny said with feeling.

'So did I,' Vicky was surprised that this adult felt the same way she did about those tense, formal dinners.

'The order of society indeed!' They both laughed. Jenny looked at Vicky closely.

'Why don't we go for a good long ride tomorrow morning? You can ride Beauty if you like.'

'Oh I'd love to,' Vicky enthused.

Jenny paused. 'I want to be a friend, Victoria. Not just a stepmother.'

'Thank you . . . Jenny.'

Well, that was a small victory, Jenny thought, at least she's calling me by name now.

'Mind you, Beauty's not an easy horse to manage.

42

Perhaps you should try a pony first.'

Vicky was indignant. 'I haven't been on a pony since I was nine years old! And anyway, I know I can handle Black Beauty . . . '

Vicky broke off her protest, seeing Jenny's teasing smile. She'd been well taken in. She couldn't help laughing herself.

'Your father told me you and Black Beauty have already become acquainted – don't worry, I'm glad. I think it means we can all become friends. Well, I'll see you tomorrow morning. Goodnight, then.'

'Goodnight, Jenny.'

Vicky moved off upstairs but, before she'd reached the first landing, the dining room doors were flung open, spitting out an angry Lord Fordham and an equally incensed Nigel Denning.

'It will be a condition of the agreement,' Fordham yelled.

But Nigel turned on him. 'My daughter is not for sale,' he lashed back, slamming his fist into his palm for emphasis.

Then, for the first time, both men became aware of Jenny's icy presence in the hall. They stopped, trying to understand the cause of her disapproval. The sound of running footsteps made it all too clear – they looked up to see Vicky sprinting up the rest of the stairs to her room.

Nigel started to go after her, but Jenny held him back. He shot one last deadly glance at Lord Fordham, before snatching at his hat and coat and storming out of the door, with Jenny following him.

Lord Fordham watched them go, then turned back in towards his study. 'Damn,' he said, 'to everyone and everything.'

6

Lord Fordham sat alone in his study, thinking over the events of the past few days. He could see what was happening. Victoria would soon be lost to him.

He kept telling himself he only wanted what was best for her. But deep down he knew that the person he was really worried about was himself. It had been hard enough losing his only daughter, but to gain a grandchild and have her taken away so quickly . . . it would be too much to bear.

But beneath his gruff exterior, he was a good man. And he had decided. He would let Victoria make up her own mind. A daughter should be with her father – he, more than anyone, knew that. He would do his utmost to persuade Victoria but, he promised, the final decision would be left to her.

The hall clock struck midnight, rousing Fordham from his private thoughts. He took a last sip from his glass of brandy which had been sitting, ignored, on his desk, and called for Finlayson.

At night the manor became as eerie as it was imposing during the day. Hollow, echoing draughts of wind raced along the empty halls, creating sounds which reverberated through the darkness. You couldn't be sure where they started or finished.

Upstairs, the floorboards creaked. A shadowy, cloaked figure appeared at the top of the stairs. It was Vicky. She edged forward cautiously, feeling her way, clutching a large unlit carrying lantern in one hand and her riding crop in the other.

When she reached the landing, voices sounded from her grandfather's study. They were moving closer. Vicky looked around wildly, searching for somewhere to hide. A huge stuffed bear – one of Lord Fordham's prize hunting trophies – stood fiercely on the landing. Vicky darted behind it. The hairy beast would easily conceal her from view . . . now, if only she could stop herself from sneezing!

Lord Fordham appeared in the lobby, still holding his brandy. Finlayson, the loyal butler, followed at his side.

'You can bolt up now, Finlayson,' Fordham said, and with a wave of his hand deposited the brandy glass on the hall table.

'Very good, sir,' Finlayson replied, waiting for his lordship to retire before clearing up after him.

Vicky held her breath while Finlayson slid the huge bolt across the double front doors. He disappeared downstairs to the servants' quarters and Vicky waited for a few more minutes to make sure the coast was clear before continuing her way downstairs.

Outside, her lantern lit, Vicky walked determinedly across the fields to the lakeside path. With the moon completely hidden by dark cloud, the night was pitch black, but Vicky was in no mood to let anything slow her down.

Soon she reached her destination and began poking around in the undergrowth with her riding crop. Snap! There it was, one of those vicious man-traps. Vicky tugged her riding crop free, then got down on her hands and knees and started rummaging through the leaves with her bare hands.

But there was nothing to be found. Vicky sighed and started all over again, striking another trap and stubbornly feeling her way around it. This went on for almost an hour before she found what she was after. Aaah! From deep within a pile of autumn leaves, she drew out a rifle. It was broken, but Vicky recognised it. It was one of the guns handed out to gamekeepers on Lord Fordham's estate.

'What're you doing there?' a deep voice sounded behind her. Vicky spun around, flashing her lantern at the voice's face. Barret looked down at her.

'Barret.' Vicky sounded firm, trying not to show how scared she was. 'I can't say I'm surprised to see you here. But I got here first. I've already found what you're looking for.'

'What? I don't know what you mean, Miss Victoria.'

The strong light wavered on his face, making him feel uncomfortable, and giving him an even more shifty appearance than he was blessed with already.

'You were so quick to blame Seth Craddon . . . and the gun had to be somewhere,' Victoria rounded on him. 'And I came here tonight to find out.'

'Eh?' Barret was staring at her stupidly, but Vicky could see he was worried. She started backing off down the path, keeping a safe distance from him. Then she held the gun triumphantly up to the light. 'I'm taking this to grandfather.'

'No, please! Miss Vicky!'

Barret made a despairing move towards her but tripped and fell heavily over one of the traps. Despite herself, Vicky felt sorry for him.

'All right. I'll wait till morning. But you be long gone.'

She ran off into the darkness, her lantern dancing happily beside her. There was a lot to be happy about. She had exposed Barret as the liar and cheat everyone had thought him to be. But more important, much more important, she had saved Seth Craddon from jail.

7

It was a wonderfully satisfied Vicky Denning who faced her father and grandfather the following morning.

Of course, they were both terribly embarrassed at being shown up by a twelve-year-old girl. They had blustered about over Seth Craddon's crimes, ignoring her pleas of his innocence. And it was only her perseverance that had avoided a frightful miscarriage of justice. It was no small thing, admitting their mistake.

'So,' Lord Fordham coughed into his morning cup of tea. 'It appears Barret was poaching my deer, using *my* traps!'

'All he had to do was walk up to those poor animals,' Nigel said, shaking his head at the thought. He turned the gun over in his hand. 'It must have gone off by accident when he was loading it.'

'Yes,' said Vicky, determined not to be left out of things. 'And he hid it in the one place your men would never have looked, grandfather – right on the spot where he was shot.'

'You should have come to me,' Nigel scolded her gently.

'She should have come to me,' Lord Fordham retorted.

'Would either of you have listened?'

The two men looked at each other. They both knew she was right. Though rivals for her affection, they had to laugh at the humour of it all – being put in their place by a young upstart of a girl.

Vicky walked over to Lord Fordham and gave him a light kiss on the cheek.

'Grandfather, why don't you make Seth Craddon the new underkeeper? It'd be a good step up for him, and you'd cut down on the poaching too.'

'Yes,' Fordham mulled over the idea. 'He wouldn't poach any more and he'd certainly know how to catch those that did.'

He paused, then faced Vicky with a twinkle in his eye. 'Perhaps I should give you the job?'

Vicky turned happily and was halfway out the door before she replied, teasing him, 'I'd have to stay here then, I suppose?'

Nigel and Lord Fordham looked at each other and laughed. Vicky poked her head back around the door with a mischievous grin. 'Grandfather would like you to have a look at his ankle.'

Nigel looked a bit confused. Fordham was simply embarrassed. His foot hurt like the devil, but it was hard to ask a favour from his former son-in-law.

'Ah, yes. Nigel, would you please?' Fordham waited, his pride telling him to stop but the pain telling him to go on. 'I was down at the lakeside this morning and . . .'

' . . . and he grazed himself in a trap,' Vicky finished her grandfather's sentence with a little too much enthusiasm. She tried, without success, to keep a straight face. Nigel was having just as much trouble.

'I'm only too happy to oblige, sir,' he said.

Lord Fordham grumbled his thanks. Vicky intervened.

'It's safe now. I threw the rest of them into the lake.'

'You did *what*?' Fordham exploded.

Vicky had to leave the room, she was giggling so hard. Nigel spluttered a laugh into his handkerchief.

'May I ask what is so confoundedly funny?' Fordham demanded.

'Nothing, sir. Nothing at all.'

Lord Fordham glared at the younger man, then relaxed with a rueful chuckle and put his foot up for Nigel to inspect.

'Oh get on with it, man. I expect you've got a lot to do . . . now that you're taking Victoria with you.'

Nigel looked up at Lord Fordham in disbelief.

'Well, hurry up then. I've got things to do, too. Can't hang around here all day.'

'Yes, sir,' Nigel replied, letting the news sink in.

Vicky, listening on the other side of the door, smiled in relief. Her fate was settled at last. She was going back to New Zealand!

The rest of Vicky's holiday passed quickly. She and Jenny roamed the countryside on horseback for much of the time, sharing the enjoyment of riding Black Beauty.

Slowly the barriers between them crumbled and Jenny became, as she had wished, a friend as well as a step-mother to Vicky.

The new school term was fast approaching but it was decided that Vicky should remain at Fordham Manor. Nigel Denning had made all the necessary arrangements. He would leave for New Zealand first and write to them once the farmhouse had been cleaned and refitted for the new Denning family.

Lord Fordham had not quite given up on his dream of having Vicky stay with him. He would make the odd comment or hint, hoping against hope she would change her mind. Of course, he and everyone knew she would not, but it kept life at the manor interesting and even Fordham took his failure in good humour.

However it was a sad day when Nigel left. Vicky had travelled over from the Manor to Dr Gordon's house. The driver was waiting and all Nigel's bags were packed up on the carriage roof. Vicky tried but could hardly speak – Jenny was just as upset.

'I'll have the farm in tip-top shape by the time you arrive. The new land will be broken in, and I'll have a long list of chores for you both.'

Nigel put on a brave face – it was always easier for the one who was leaving than those left behind. He hugged both Jenny and Vicky, then turned to Dr Gordon.

'God bless,' Dr Gordon said.

'Goodbye. Goodbye.'

Nigel stepped into the carriage. It started off almost immediately, too soon for Vicky and Jenny who walked behind it, keeping pace. Nigel's head poked out of the carriage window.

'In two months' time we'll be together again! Count the weeks. I'll be counting each day,' he cried out.

He waved as the horse and carriage rolled down the lane and out of sight. As the sound of its creaking wooden wheels died away, the Dennings were left in a depressing silence.

'Come on,' Dr Gordon clapped his hands suddenly to break the standstill. 'Inside, both of you. I prescribe a good strong cup of tea . . . '

But if Vicky thought she would be moping for long, she was very much mistaken. There was so much to do to get ready for their trip. Tidying up loose ends, seeing to Jenny's veterinary rounds in the surrounding district, helping Seth Craddon settle into his new job as underkeeper, it all served to take her mind off her absent father.

She was so busy she didn't really notice that Nigel had not written. Letters and travelling took such a long time in her eyes that she thought it not at all unusual. Jenny and Dr Gordon were more concerned. However they said nothing.

Lord Fordham had also been busy. He was eagerly waiting for Vicky to arrive back from yet another visit with Jenny.

'Afternoon tea when Miss Victoria returns, Finlayson,' he announced, looking very pleased with himself.

'Yes, sir,' Finlayson replied.

'And plenty of cakes . . . ' Finlayson left without another word. Lord Fordham drew a small leather box out of his desk drawer and opened it. Inside lay a beautiful and very expensive-looking pearl necklace. He held it up to the light. The pearls glowed brilliantly – not one was cloudy or flawed in any way.

Just then Vicky entered.

'Hello, grandfather.' She saw the pearls. Her mouth fell open in a breathless, 'Oh!'

'Pearls were your grandmother's favourite.' He handed them to her.

'Have these been in the family since then?' Vicky asked, curious.

'Certainly a . . . a very considerable length of time.'

Vicky looked at him dubiously. 'It's just that the box seems very new.'

Lord Fordham was caught off guard. She constantly surprised him. He wondered if she had guessed about the pearls.

'You didn't just happen to buy them in London yesterday, grandfather?' Vicky was gently disapproving.

She saw right through him. Lord Fordham could see that, there was no point in denying it.

'Victoria,' he tried to explain. 'They are a gift.'

'No grandfather, they're not,' she replied, putting him squarely in his place. 'They are a bribe.'

She handed the pearls back to him. 'Two weeks ago you had business in Italy and wanted me to go with you.'

'You like Italy,' Fordham protested.

Vicky paused, exasperated. 'Grandfather, I've made up my mind. I am going, and I won't be swayed.'

'Like your mother.' Lord Fordham was beaten. He looked dejected. 'I never saw her again.'

'I'll come back,' Vicky consoled him. 'And you'll be here when I do.'

At that Lord Fordham sighed, 'I'm not as young as I used to be, you know. And you will be gone a long while . . .'

'Grandfather, you're as strong as a horse – and as cunning as a fox. I'm not going to fall for that kind of talk.'

'What a way to address a peer of the realm,' Lord Fordham laughed. 'There's no getting around you, is there?'

'Not on this. You know me. I'm just a wild colonial lass with no manners.'

Fordham studied her with affection. He took the necklace and again tried to put it around her neck.

'This time, my dear, I mean it. As a gift.'

But Vicky held out her hand and stopped him. 'No, grandfather. But thank you.'

A dinner gong sounded in the next room.

'Ah . . . tea,' said Fordham, rubbing his hands together. 'There's a chocolate cake as well. Would that count as a bribe, do you think?'

'Yes I think it would,' Vicky laughed. 'But this once I'll overlook it!'

Lord Fordham followed Vicky out through the

library door, chuckling to himself. He had lost the war, but what an opponent! Vicky Denning, he was happy to boast, was truly a worth heir to the Fordham legacy.

8

Vicky rode up to Dr Gordon's house on Lord Fordham's grey mare. It was her turn to ride Black Beauty today, and she was looking forward to it.

When she arrived, there was no-one else to be seen, so she went happily around the back and saddled up the big black horse. As she rode back to the cottage entrance, she could hear voices.

Ahead of her, Jenny and Dr Gordon were standing in front of the house. They did not seem to hear her as she cantered to a halt beside them.

'Ready for a ride?'

Jenny turned sharply, her eyes filled with tears. In her hand she held a crumpled piece of paper. A telegram. Vicky was startled and becoming scared. Dr Gordon held out his hand.

'Would you like to get down, my dear?'

'Why? What's happened?'

'It might be better if we talk in the house.'

'What? What is it?'

Dr Gordon started to say something, but Jenny cut in before he could speak. She rattled the words off quickly, as if they hurt too much to think about.

'Your father's ship is overdue at Singapore . . . it's . . . it's been reported missing.'

Dr Gordon lifted his hand again. 'Vicky,' he said softly, 'Come down.'

Vicky barely noticed him. She was staring at Jenny, reading the emotion on her face. 'It's more than that, isn't it?'

Jenny took a deep breath. 'They've found some wreckage.'

'No!' Vicky shook her head violently. She wouldn't listen to this, she told herself, it wasn't happening.

'Please, my dear, calm yourself.' Dr Gordon looked worried.

'No! It's not true!' Vicky yelled again. She wheeled Black Beauty around and galloped off at speed. Jenny began to run towards the stables, but her father held her back.

'No. Let her go.'

Vicky rode Black Beauty as hard as she had ever ridden in her life. He seemed to sense her distress, and his hooves fairly flew over the ground as he stretched out to full gallop. Even when they reached thick forest, the pace barely slackened – Black Beauty swerved and dodged the trees and low branches with practised ease.

All of a sudden, though, Beauty pulled to a halt, whinnying loudly. The abrupt stop shook Vicky out of her thoughts. In front of her, brandishing a long, heavy stick, was Barret.

'I hear you're leaving us, Miss Victoria.' Barret sounded nastier than ever. Vicky blinked. After the news about her father, she hadn't properly taken in his presence. Barret mistook her silence for fear. He moved closer.

'I thought you might like to say goodbye.' He raised the stick back, ready to strike.

'Get out of my way, Barret,' Vicky warned. She was in no mood for this.

'Let's see how fine you look off that horse.' But as Barret moved in, Black Beauty reared up on his hind legs, snorting in anger. Barret had to leap to one side to avoid being injured, and he fell heavily.

'Get out of my way, or I'll ride you down,' Vicky shouted, her voice blazing with fury. She turned

Beauty around to face the fallen man. Like most cowards, the fight had gone out of him at the first sign of a skirmish.

'Don't,' he cried. 'Don't hurt me!'

Vicky brought Beauty easily under control. 'I'm not scared of you, Barret,' she cautioned him. 'I told you once before to leave. I won't tell you again.'

Barret stumbled to his feet, keeping a wary eye on the fiery black horse. This time Vicky bluffed him – pretending to charge again, but backing off at the last minute. Barret, however, did not wait to find out. He scurried away through the thicket, out of Fordham country for good.

Vicky watched him go. Then, once she was sure he was not coming back, she slumped over in the saddle, weeping silently at the thought of her father lost at sea.

Black Beauty stood nervously – pacing a step one way then the other – concerned about his young rider. Soon Vicky half slid and half dismounted to the ground, where she sat still holding the reins. Her weeping grew louder until deep sobs filled the gloomy shadows of the forest. Beauty leaned forward, nuzzling her with his nose, trying to console her.

After almost an hour, Jenny arrived on Fordham's grey mare. She joined Vicky, seated on the grass. For some time, neither one spoke. Finally, Vicky turned to face her step-mother.

'I'm sorry I just rode off like that.'

'I understand. When my mother died, I went and hid in the attic for hours.'

The pair fell back into an uneasy silence. When Jenny spoke again, she was quiet and determined.

'I'm going to change the route and stop in Singapore before Sydney. That's the closest port to . . . to where it happened.'

Vicky was equally determined. 'I'm coming with you.'

'No, Vicky. You don't have to do this.'

'But yes, I do. You must see that. I have to go with you, no matter what happens,' Vicky was desperate, pleading. 'Jenny, I want to go home.'

They looked at each other. Inside they had been torn apart by the events of that day. They shared an understanding which nobody else could ever be part of, and it united them. From now on, they belonged together.

The next few days were so busy there was no time for grief. Both Jenny and Vicky avoided the well-meaning locals who came offering their condolences. They finished packing for the long trip ahead, ignoring Lord Fordham and an equally concerned Dr Gordon who felt the women would be better off staying at home until they knew for certain of Nigel's fate.

'I can't sit here, not knowing – not *doing* anything,' Jenny shot back at them. 'Vicky can't either. She's not a Fordham and I'm not Jenny Gordon any longer, I'm a Denning. We are both Dennings, and we will sort this out together.'

With their minds made up, there was little the elder men could do to stop them. Soon the day came to say goodbye. Jenny had saved a special time that morning to spend with Black Beauty. True, some horses had survived round-the-world voyages, but the risks for a horse of Beauty's age were just too great. He deserved to spend the rest of his life in peace amidst the rolling English countryside he knew and trusted.

Jenny cantered out into a nearby field and dismounted. She stood talking to Beauty for a long time, stopping occasionally to feed another sugar lump into his mouth. Finally, near tears, she threw her arms around his neck, giving him a tight hug.

'Goodbye, my Beauty . . . .'

She stepped back, then turned and without looking behind her, walked quickly to where the others were waiting.

Vicky and Jenny were fitted out for the journey – each with scarf, gloves and hat. The driver was packing the last of their bags as Jenny arrived. Lord Fordham had come over from the Manor to Dr Gordon's and was bent down on one knee, saying his last goodbyes to Vicky.

'Now you promise to come back?'

'Of course I will, grandfather. You know I will – this is my second home,' she looked at him fondly. 'Thank you . . . for everything.'

They hugged, as Jenny and her father went through the same sad partings.

'I'll look after Beauty. You needn't worry about him,' Dr Gordon said quietly.

'I know you will. Thank you, father.'

She turned to Lord Fordham. 'Goodbye, sir.'

'Goodbye,' Fordham coughed, still not sure of how to address this new member of his family. 'Goodbye . . . Jennifer.'

Jenny smiled her thanks and followed Vicky into the trap. Before any of them could think, the driver cracked his whip, and they were away.

'Goodbye!' Vicky cried, as they clattered off down the drive.

'Goodbye,' Dr Gordon replied, waving farewell. Lord Fordham was quite silent next to him. From the corner of his eye, Dr Gordon saw the crusty old man wipe his hand across his face, trying to hide the tears.

'Try this,' he said softly, offering Fordham a handkerchief.

'Much obliged, doctor.' He blew his nose. They both stood watching the horse and trap fade off into the distance. Lord Fordham was the first to turn away, but Dr Gordon lingered a while longer.

'God speed you both,' he whispered.

Vicky was possessed with a curious sense of freedom. She leaned out the window, allowing the breeze to wash over her face. Their preparations for travel had been touched with an inescapable feeling of sadness following news of the shipwreck. But now, once they had set out, she felt happier and more optimistic than ever about their chances of finding her father.

As they rounded a corner in the road, she saw a figure standing, blocking their path. Soon she could make out who it was – Seth Craddon. She signalled the driver to stop.

'Seth. It's goodbye today, I'm afraid.'

Seth Craddon doffed his cap. 'Goodbye, Miss Vicky. God bless.'

Jenny leaned forward in her seat. 'Mr Craddon, I hear you and Mr Barret had an argument . . . and he lost.'

'He lost a couple of teeth too, ma'am,' Seth grinned, and turned to Vicky. 'I'm glad to see you're going home, miss. It's where we all should be.'

From behind his back, he brought out a small bunch of wild primroses. Vicky took them and smiled her thanks. Jenny motioned to the driver, and they were off again on their way.

They trundled along the country roads, past fields which took them ever nearer to the local railway station. Suddenly Vicky pointed out alongside the trap.

'Look!'

There, galloping at full stretch, parallel to their trap, was Black Beauty. Having caught up with them, he measured their pace, stride for stride, then broke away and dashed to the top of the hill – rearing majestically on his hind legs in a final goodbye to his friends.

Jenny was caught between pleasure and sadness. But Vicky was thrilled at the sight. 'We'll be all right,' she said, patting Jenny on the arm. 'Black Beauty will always be with us.'

Jenny smiled. Vicky was so confident and trusting, she thought. She hoped that the girl would not become downhearted if things did not turn out the way they planned.

9

Jenny's decision to go to Singapore had not been a success. They had stayed in an English hotel and received every assistance from those in charge of the search for Nigel's ship. But nothing more had been heard; no further wreckage or survivors had been sighted.

After six weeks, Jenny felt at a loss. There was nothing more they could do. Since arriving, everyone had been telling her to return home to England. They had been understanding at first, but her continued presence made them feel a little uncomfortable. She could sense she had acquired a reputation as a 'crank'. People began avoiding her and Vicky as they went about the colony, searching for news or clues of Nigel's ship.

Finally, she had to agree with those around her. She couldn't stay in Singapore for ever, especially with a young girl to look after. But she couldn't go back. Her life in England had changed once she met Nigel, and it would never be the same. Even if he was dead, she couldn't just give up on that part of her life and go home as if nothing had happened.

They would go on to New Zealand, as planned. First, however, was the stopover in Sydney, Australia.

In a new city, Jenny and Vicky redoubled their efforts to find out the fate of Nigel's lost ship. This time, their contact was a Mr Chambers, manager of the Sydney branch of the Bank of England. He was a neat little man, middle-aged and balding, with an irritating habit of rubbing his fingernails together as he talked.

'I can only say what you already know,' he told them in his best banking manner, bland and very precise. 'Some of the lifeboats were unaccounted for, so yes, there may be some survivors. But natives in the region have been known to take people captive . . . '

He's almost enjoying it, thought Vicky, who had taken an instant dislike to the man. But she was wrong. Mr Chambers was more used to doing business with men. The sight of the two Denning women in his office had really put him quite on edge. If the truth were known, he would have preferred to have seen them at his home. That would have been much more appropriate, he felt. But there they were, sitting in front of him. He'd just have to deal with them as quickly as possible so they would leave with least fuss.

Jenny, however, wasn't having any of that rubbish. She rummaged about in her handbag and brought out a sheet of paper, which she handed to him.

'This is a notice asking for any news of my husband to be forwarded to New Zealand. It's all in the Far East newspapers.'

Mr Chambers took it, nodding vigorously.

'I want it in all the Australian papers as well. You'll handle that for me?'

'Uh . . . yes, of course. For how long?' Mr Chambers looked grave, as if this simple request was full of difficulties.

'Until otherwise instructed.' Jenny's answer was firm and to the point, but Mr Chambers couldn't see that.

'Mrs Denning, I must tell you . . . '

Vicky, who had been sitting quietly all this time, suddenly interrupted. 'Mr Chambers, I should tell you that my grandfather has a large account with this bank. He would not be happy if he thought you weren't doing your best to help us.'

Mr Chambers just stared at Vicky, open-mouthed. She returned his stern gaze until he was quite unsure what to do next.

'Yes, I see,' he said, doubtfully. 'Well, I'll see about some tea, then, shall I?'

He left the room. Jenny was tightlipped – Vicky could see that she didn't approve of the way she had treated Mr Chambers.

'I'm sorry,' Vicky said, at last. 'But don't you see? They've already decided. They think Daddy is . . .'

She couldn't bring herself to say the words.

'But *we* haven't,' Jenny said adamantly. 'We still believe he's alive, don't we? There's always got to be hope. And if he does come back, we've got to be where he knows he'll find us. We have to go home – to New Zealand – and we should go there now, before winter closes the roads.'

Vicky smiled ruefully. 'Jenny, there aren't any roads where we're going.'

From Australia they sailed across the Tasman Sea to New Zealand, travelling up river from Auckland, north to the tiny settlement called Puhoi (Poo-hoy) where the Denning farm was situated.

The night before they arrived, Vicky and Jenny camped out under the stars with two drovers who were their guides for the journey. The Denning women huddled together, wrapping blankets around them for warmth against the cold night air.

Jenny looked up. 'Is that the Southern Cross?' she asked.

Vicky nodded. 'Yes, the stars here are completely different to England.'

'They seem much brighter,' Jenny replied. 'But then everything seems different from home.'

As she spoke, they heard a sudden grunting sound close by.

'What's that?' Jenny jumped, startled at the sound.

'Oh no – it's a wild pig,' Vicky leapt up. 'Quick, they're dangerous.'

'What!' Jenny looked about, terrified. Then she saw Vicky was laughing at her, and pointing across the campfire. The sound was coming from one of the drovers, snoring as he slept. Jenny pulled a face.

'Goodnight, you little rascal.'

'Goodnight,' Vicky said, still laughing. 'It's really not that bad here – once you get used to it.'

After Vicky had fallen asleep, Jenny lay awake thinking. There was something different about New Zealand. The air was so clean and the light so fresh and bright, she felt she could almost reach out and touch it.

The country felt young and full of possibility. It made Jenny feel really alive but she was also scared at the unfamiliarity of it all, and she was glad that Vicky was there to help. Thoughts of Vicky brought the image of Nigel racing back to her. He was seldom out of her thoughts, but she knew that they would have to start their new life in the colonies as if he was never to return. Jenny had never been so sad, but the idea of a fresh start in a new country also excited her and she went to sleep with all sorts of dreams racing around her head.

Such thoughts soon evaporated the next day. New Zealand may have seemed romantic and exciting at night, but it certainly lacked many of the home comforts. They were trekking miles over roughly-hewn roads by horse and dray – a long slung cart which jolted them around on its roughcut wooden seats.

By mid-afternoon on their fourth day in New Zealand, the cart took them into a remote valley. Its dense, green native bush had been completely cleared – wiped out in one of the massive land burn-offs, which often broke the land itself.

In the absence of anything else, clumps of tussock-like maram grass had sprung up. Elsewhere, the odd native fern or cabbage tree dotted the scene.

The track through the valley led to the Puhoi valley settlement, just a few small weatherbeaten huts and a general store with the proud sign 'Grocer & Post Office' painted in its window.

Vicky and Jenny got down from the cart.

'Can you have everything up to the farm by tomorrow?' Jenny asked the drover.

'Aye Miss,' he replied. 'No worries at all.'

Vicky turned to Jenny. 'But we can go on, can't we? We can get some horses here and be at the farm well before dark.'

'Could I stop you?' Jenny asked, then answered her own question, saying 'I think it's a very good idea. Off you go.'

Vicky smiled her thanks and rushed off behind the store to see her old friend Mr Forbes, the local blacksmith. There he was, leaning over his forge, working on yet another horseshoe.

'Mr Forbes,' Vicky said, breathless as she approached, 'Hello Mr Forbes, it's me, Vicky.'

'Mr Forbes' looked up and pulled off his cap. Vicky was stunned. It wasn't Mr Forbes at all, in fact it wasn't even a man! Puhoi now had a woman 'smithy'. She looked a bit cross, Vicky thought.

'Oh,' she ventured politely. 'Isn't Mr Forbes here any more?'

'No,' the woman replied gruffly, and didn't say any more.

'Um . . . we want to hire two horses, please.'

'Right then, I'll saddle 'em up.'

'Thank you,' Vicky replied, but the woman didn't move. She just stood there, staring.

'You can go and settle up inside.'

'Oh, yes . . . of course.'

Jenny was already there, waiting to be served. The store, the only one in the district, was stocked full of everything you'd ever think you needed.

On the main counter, Vicky could see row upon row of large glass jars containing brightly coloured sweets. Deep shelves lined the shop from floor to ceiling and large sacks of different grains, flour, salt and sugar were stacked neatly in one corner.

The right hand counter was given over to the Post Office, where the shopkeeper was taking mail from a couple of shearers. He dealt with them, then walked around to the shop counter to serve Jenny and Vicky.

'Yes,' he said, removing his postmaster's cap. 'Now this list you've given me . . . '

'Yes?' Jenny replied.

The man studied it, frowning. 'It'll have to be tomorrow . . . '

'That's all right, Mr . . . ?'

'My name's Samuel Burton. I'm going to need some money on account.'

Surprised, Jenny took out her purse. Maybe this was the way people did things in the colonies. Vicky knew better.

'Mr Forbes never made us pay in advance.'

'Young lady, Mr Forbes went bankrupt twelve months ago. I'll not follow him down that sorry road. Ten shillings please.'

'Don't forget the hire on the horses,' Jenny said. She was irritated – she'd show him who was honest. Burton was caught a bit off balance by her approach, but he recovered quickly.

'Ah . . . no, I hadn't. That's five shillings extra, thank you. Are you going straight to the farm, Mrs Denning?'

'Yes, we are. By the way, have you seen much of the overseer Mr Steadman?'

'Can't say I have at that,' Burton looked knowingly over at the two shearers who had stayed to watch the new arrivals. 'Or his assistant, either.'

'Mr Grimwald?'

'Yes,' Burton said slowly, 'Mr *Grimwald*.' He put a particular emphasis on 'Grimwald' as if there was something quite odd about him. Jenny chose to ignore the comment. Just then the woman blacksmith, Hilda Burton, came in beside her husband at the counter.

'Your horses are ready.'

Jenny and Vicky thanked them and left. Even before they were out the door, Hilda whispered in her husband's ear, 'Did you tell them about the farm?'

Samuel Burton shrugged. 'None of my business, is it?' He dropped Jenny's money in the cash register and slammed the door shut.

10

This last leg of their journey was much easier. Riding on horseback together reminded them of home, even if the surroundings were very different. They had almost reached the top of a small hill.

'You can see our farm from over the rise. Come on, Jenny!'

She kicked the horse into a canter. Jenny followed and they galloped up, eager for the first sight of their new home.

'There!' Vicky shouted, her face flushed with excitement. Jenny reined in alongside her, taking in the farm homestead and its buildings (a large barn and shearers' shed) below. From their distance it looked a cosy haven from the rest of wild and rugged country. The main house was surrounded on three sides by a wide verandah. And Jenny could see it had been built to make the most of its enchanting setting. Each morning, when the sun rose in the east, the house would be bathed in light on its front two sides. At night, from the western aspect, they could sit outside and watch the sunset glowing out to sea.

'So this is home,' she said quietly. Vicky, however, wasn't listening. She was looking ahead, concern showing on her face.

'Something's wrong,' she said. 'I can feel it.'

As they neared the homestead, Vicky's fears proved correct. It was like an American ghost town. They rode through the entrance unchecked – the gate was off its hinges – and circled the house, taking stock of the mess which stood before them.

Doors opening on to the verandah slammed open and shut in the wind, broken furniture lay scattered about both inside and outside the house. The whole farm looked unkempt and uncared for. Even the roses, which Vicky's mother had so lovingly cherished, had run wild. Some were broken; most were dead. It broke Vicky's heart to see them like this.

'We had animals here . . . chickens . . . pigs . . . two cows and some sheep. Four horses.' She looked around, but nothing moved. 'Marigold the goose . . . they were all here. They were all my friends.'

Jenny thought for a moment. 'Mr Steadman and Mr Grimwald appear to have left. And that man at the shop, Burton, he knew it, I'm sure. Come on, let's see what it's like inside.'

They pushed hard against the back door and it finally gave way, sending them inside through a mass of cobwebs which had built up since the house was abandoned.

'Ughh . . . ' Vicky was repulsed. It was as if she was a stranger in her own house, she thought. It felt spooky and she didn't like it, but nothing prepared her for the sight which greeted them when they reached the kitchen.

The long kitchen table looked as though it had been left in the middle of a meal which had long since been eaten by rats. Plates and utensils were scattered about and there was dust everywhere. But the rats hadn't left – there were three scurrying around on the benches. One darted out of the door between Vicky's legs. She jumped back, then:

'How dare they leave our home like this!' she exploded.

Jenny sighed wearily. Really, it seemed like the last straw. This was not what she had expected. But there was nothing else for it – they would have to get stuck in and make it work. They only had themselves to rely on now and, no matter how bad things got, she couldn't let Vicky think that they were beaten.

She clapped her hands together and put on a brave face. 'There's nothing here that a good clean-up won't fix. You get the horses stabled; I'll start a fire.'

Vicky nodded and raced outside, glad to be clear of the musty house. Half-way to the barn the huge door swung open, creaking loudly. But Vicky thought she could hear something else. She crept forward slowly. There it was again – a sort of clanking.

'Is somebody there?' But her request was met with silence. She hesitated, then burst inside the building, loudly demanding, 'Who's there?'

From high above her a weird contraption seemed to fly down, making straight for her head. She ducked just in time and screamed, as the device sailed past, crashing into a far wall.

From inside the house, Jenny heard Vicky's cry of panic. She dropped the firewood and ran for the door. She found Vicky standing over the weird contrivance – neither of them had ever seen anything like it.

'What is it?' Jenny asked, confused.

From deep within the barnyard gloom, they heard a rustling noise, then the sound of someone coughing. A strange goggled figure strode towards them.

He took off his goggles and examined the machine. 'It is for flying,' he said, in a thick German accent. 'I make it fly.'

The man had turned out to be not much older than a boy – about eighteen years old, Vicky thought, and good-looking in a dreamy absent minded way. He also seemed quite shy, not sure how to act in front of the two women before him.

'Who are you?' Vicky asked.

'Oh, I am sorry. I am Manfred. Manfred Bayer. How do you do?' He extended a dirty hand to Vicky then Jenny. 'Can I be of help?'

While Jenny put Manfred to work in the house, Vicky slipped outside. There was something she had to do. Something she had promised solemnly she would do as soon as she returned home.

She crossed a nearby field and headed down a gentle slope to a grotto of trees. Despite its low-lying position, there was still a clear view between two hills to the jet black sand dunes and blue, crashing sea. This had been her mother's favourite place, and it was where she now lay buried.

Vicky knelt down beside the marble headstone and re-read the inscription as if it was only yesterday she had last been there.

'Sacred to the Memory of
SARAH
Beloved wife of NIGEL DENNING
and
Mother to VICTORIA
December 12, 1900'

The grave was well tended, with fresh flowers sitting in a vase by the headstone. Vicky picked at the grass and lightly touched the flowers.

'I miss you, mother,' she whispered softly.

A horse whinny in the distance interrupted her thoughts. She looked up. On a massive sand dune away from the homestead, she could see a magnificent black stallion.

Behind her, Jenny was calling. Vicky turned and waved. When she looked back, the horse was gone. Mystified, she sat back down beside her mother's grave for a few quiet moments before heading back to the house.

Inside, a great deal of work had been done. Jenny was surprised. She had actually been right, most of the mess was just surface dirt and clutter – it hadn't been too hard to clean up. Now with a fire going and Manfred working very hard, scrubbing the floors and cutting more firewood, the kitchen, at least, was taking on a very homely appearance.

Manfred placed a couple more logs in the stove fire and edged nervously towards Jenny. 'Mr Steadman said the farm is sold. So the stock, he said, must go. He said I can stay until the new owner comes.'

'Why didn't you stay in here?' Vicky asked him.

'It is not my house. I am happy outside – I sleep in the open sometimes. I like that.' Manfred paused, thinking things through. 'Mr Steadman was not honest, I think.'

Jenny nodded her head. 'You're right – he was not.'

Vicky was studying Manfred closely. She had decided he was a good person. 'Was it you who looked after my mother's grave?' she queried.

Manfred nodded. 'Thank you,' Vicky told him.

Now it was Jenny's turn to size the young man up. 'So,' she said, 'you've been here on your own, building a flying machine?'

'Yes. My design will use natural power . . . from the body, from the air. Like a bird.'

'Without an engine?' Vicky found all this very hard to believe.

'Birds do not need an engine. What they can do, we can do. One day, I will show you.' Manfred was quite excited but he suddenly held his hand up, stopping in midstream. 'Oh, I forget. A letter comes before you arrive. It is from England.'

He reached into his shirt pocket and took out a crumpled envelope which he gave to Jenny. Her face lit up.

'It's from father!' Vicky watched, excited, as Jenny tore open the letter. Overhead, a roll of thunder sounded and rain began to patter down. Jenny read the first lines eagerly, then her face fell.

'What is it?' Vicky tried to read what Dr Gordon had written, but Jenny began reading out loud.

'Dearest Jenny . . . I hope this letter finds you and Vicky well. My reason for writing so soon, however, is very sad. Black Beauty is no more . . . '

Vicky gasped. It couldn't be true. Jenny continued, blinking back tears.

'He died a week after you left. It was very peaceful. We have put him in the back of the north field, by the trees. Part of my life has ended and I know part of yours. A very great and loving part . . . '

Jenny was overcome, unable to read any further. Vicky put her arm around Jenny's shoulder. They were both crying now, not only for that wonderful horse but for everything that had led them half-way across the world – bad luck dogging them every step.

The rain started to pelt down, but above the heavy deluge they heard a sharp stamping outside the house. Vicky ran to the door, Jenny following with the lantern and Manfred bringing up the rear.

They all saw it at once. Framed against the darkness and sleeting rain was a big black horse.

'Where did he come from?' Jenny murmured. Manfred shook his head.

'I have never seen him before.'

But Vicky had. She stepped out into the rain towards the frightened animal. He had a white star mark on his forehead, just like Black Beauty. A frayed rope was still strapped tight around his neck

– someone had tried to tame him, but had ill-treated him in the process.

'It's all right, boy,' said Vicky, her arm out-stretched. 'I'm not going to hurt you. My name is Vicky, who are you?'

The horse reared up nervously, stamping its fore-legs back down hard on the ground. He made an impressive sight.

'Take it slowly,' Jenny called out. Vicky acknowl-edged her but didn't turn around. She kept talking quietly and edging closer to the stallion. She saw some marks on his flank.

'Somebody's tried to hurt you, haven't they, boy? We won't hurt you. You are all right with us. You know that, too, don't you?'

One more step and she was near enough to grab hold of the rope. She reached up, letting him sniff her hand, then she let her hands stray cautiously down his neck. She patted him with one hand, while the other closed softly around the rope.

Neither Vicky nor the horse moved. Looking on, Manfred was delighted.

'Oh,' he said to Jenny. 'He is a great horse, yes?'

'Yes,' Jenny replied. 'A beautiful, black horse.'

Vicky turned to her and smiled. 'A beauty . . . Black Beauty.'

11

That night in bed, Vicky was exhilarated. She had no idea how she would manage to sleep. A horse like that of her very own! It really seemed to trust her. When Manfred had tried to get close, it had reared and snorted disconcertedly – even with Jenny he wasn't exactly comfortable.

Vicky tossed and turned. What she had really wanted was to spend her first night back at Puhoi in the barn with the new Black Beauty, but Jenny had said 'No' in a voice that wasn't to be argued with.

It was light when Vicky woke the next morning. That she had slept at all surprised her – but, more than that, she was late! Jenny and Manfred had already been up for three hours. Jenny said that Vicky had been overtired and needed to catch up. Vicky didn't believe her. She knew there was only one thing she needed to catch up with – her wonderful new horse.

She raced out to the barn and began feeding Beauty some grass, patting him gently. Jenny walked in.

'He's still a bit nervous,' Vicky told her in a low voice. 'But he's better than last night . . . I think he likes me.'

'I can see he does. You're a lucky girl.' Jenny stopped and surveyed the barn, her eyes coming to rest on Manfred's flying machine.

'What a contraption. Does Manfred really think he can fly it?'

Vicky wasn't listening, she still had all her attention on Black Beauty.

'Where do you think he's from?'

'What, Manfred? Germany,' Jenny replied.

'I meant Black Beauty.'

They laughed at this small misunderstanding – it was their first agreeable moment since arriving 'home'.

'Well, I expect one of the older stallions tried to force him out of the herd. There are a nice set of teethmarks on his flank. And a ropemark. Somebody's tried to tame him.'

'They didn't do a very nice job. There'll be no more rope marks from now on.'

'Come on, you young horse trainer,' Jenny urged. 'Breakfast. You can't operate on an empty stomach, and he'll still be here when you get back.'

They walked back together to the homestead. 'Manfred's nice, isn't he,' Vicky pondered aloud. 'We should ask him to stay.'

'I know, but what are we to pay him with – fresh air?'

Now that they were here, the harsh realities were beginning to set in. Jenny tried to lighten things.

'Let's just see if he can cook, shall we?'

Oh dear! The minute Jenny and Vicky reached the kitchen, Manfred sat them down and slopped several thick globs of oatmeal into two bowls in front of them.

'Porridge,' he announced proudly. 'And some milk I got from the next farm before you woke up. Please . . . eat.'

He turned back to the oven and kept on talking. 'Some water got in last night, but I will fix the roof after breakfast.'

Vicky and Jenny exchanged looks. Vicky picked up her spoon and stuck it fast into her porridge. It stayed standing upright. Jenny tried hard to keep a straight face, she even attempted eating a small mouthful when Manfred turned around to watch. Her face went rigid under Manfred's gaze. She swallowed the food, and managed a feeble smile but, as soon as Manfred went back to his task, she drank a great draught of the milk to take away the taste.

Manfred had now prepared the second course. He placed a plate of flat, black 'somethings' on the table with a flourish.

'Oh, is this a colonial recipe of some sort,' Jenny asked politely.

'It is toast.'

'Oh,' Vicky and Jenny said together. This time they couldn't hide their embarrassment at his efforts. Manfred was puzzled and hurt – he had always enjoyed his own cooking.

Jenny patted his hand. 'Thank you very much, Manfred. All this, everything you've done – it's wonderful.'

Now it was Manfred's turn to be embarrassed. He grinned bashfully. 'I am glad. Now I go and repair the roof.'

He raced outside, leaving Jenny and Vicky free to collapse in laughter. 'I'll say one thing for him,' Jenny gasped. 'He does have energy.'

'I think he'd like to stay,' Vicky offered. 'I wish we could afford to keep him here.'

'We've got to get our stock back first. We don't have the money to replace it – and without the animals, this farm can't pay for itself.'

It didn't look promising. Vicky thought for a moment. 'Grandfather could send us the money,' she said suddenly. 'Shall I write to him?'

Jenny studied her for a long time before replying. 'This is our problem,' she said evenly. 'Not his. We will solve it our way, together.'

Vicky could have kissed her. It was the exact answer she had wanted to hear.

Manfred spent most of the day clambering up and down the corrugated iron roof. Whole sections of it had broken away, but a hammer and a boxful of nails seemed to do the trick.

Vicky, of course, spent her time walking Black Beauty around the small front paddock. Jenny came out to watch, bringing Manfred a cup of tea for his efforts.

Manfred was one of life's naturally exuberant characters. Nothing ever appeared to get him down-hearted. He bounced off the ladder and collected his cup of tea with a beaming smile.

'That should fix the leaks for some time. In the colonies, you need to be practical. It is a good place to try out new things . . .'

'Like your flying machine? Have you ever flown in it?'

'No. Not yet, but I will. It is not a dream.'

Jenny was impressed. Vicky is right, she thought, he is a good man. 'I'm sure it's no dream, Manfred.'

A shriek from the front paddock sent them running. They found Vicky, sprawled on the ground and Beauty quietly standing against a fence watching her.

'Are you all right?' Manfred asked, reaching her first.

Vicky just nodded and scrambled to her feet, reaching again for Beauty's rope harness.

'You didn't try to ride him, did you?' Jenny's voice was sharp and accusing.

'Well . . . I just got on and off.'

'Yes, you got off rather quickly, didn't you?'

Vicky looked shamefaced, but Jenny wasn't about to let her off that lightly. 'If you try riding an unbroken horse, you'll find yourself flying through the air long before Manfred does.'

Vicky didn't say anything for a while, but it was obvious she understood. 'I will be able to ride Beauty soon though, won't I?' she pleaded.

'In time. It's like anything, you get better results with patience.'

Jenny went back into the house. Manfred finished his tea and gave Vicky a reassuring smile before disappearing into the barn to work on his flying machine.

Vicky approached Black Beauty again. 'It's all right, Beauty. I don't mind. But next time you won't throw me with everyone watching, will you? Promise you won't, and I'll get you some sugar lumps in town.'

Black Beauty nuzzled up close to Vicky's face.

Way off on a distant hill, someone else has been watching the proceedings with interest. Frank Coates, the hardbitten landowner from the next valley, sat astride his horse observing the fresh activity at the Denning farm through a small telescope.

He waited until Vicky had led Black Beauty inside the barn. Then he sat for a while, as if considering his next move, before riding away without announcing his presence.

Manfred was only too happy to be left behind while Jenny and Vicky went back to the settlement. He didn't like the locals much – they thought he was strange with his German accent and, once they had heard about his crazy inventions, they treated him more as if he were the local madman than a serious inventor.

For Vicky and Jenny, however, it was important that they get themselves established. Manfred had given them the name of the local police constable to report the missing livestock, and they needed to pick up some more supplies to tide them over the next few weeks.

They dismounted outside the store, and tethered their horses to the hitching rail.

Vicky nudged Jenny and pointed across the road. 'There he is,' she said, pointing to a very young, very serious-looking man in a police uniform. It was Constable Carmody. He, too, had dismounted and was about to look at his horse's hoof.

'I'll talk to him,' Jenny said, handing over the supplies' list to Vicky. 'See if Mr Burton will add these to our order.'

'You know, Burton knew we had nothing at the farm. He took our money and probably hoped we wouldn't come back.'

'You don't know that, so you be polite to him,' Jenny said in a warning tone.

'Oh! Can't I be just a bit rude?' Vicky teased.

'No you cannot.' Jenny pretended to be shocked. She broke away suddenly and crossed the road towards Constable Carmody.

'Constable . . . I'm Mrs Denning.'

The young constable straightened. 'Yes ma'am, how can I be of assistance?' He spoke in a lilting Irish brogue, and held a penknife in one hand, about to remove a stone from his horse's hoof.

'Well first, perhaps I could be of assistance to you?' Jenny examined the horse's foreleg and held out her hand for the knife.

Vicky watched all this with a smile. She liked to see men's reactions to Jenny's skills. But she had to face Mr Burton. She was just about to 'get it over with', when she spied a farmer tying his horse and cart up outside the store. There was a sick calf lying in the back.

Vicky approached it. 'Hello little fellow, what's the matter with you?'

'He's poisoned, Missy . . . him and all the others. I thought the vet'inary could have a look at him.'

'The veterinary?'

'Mr Burton,' the farmer explained. 'He does for us around here.'

So that was it, thought Vicky, Mr Burton seems to do everything around here that would make him some money.

'Is he qualified?' she asked innocently.

'No, but he's all there is.'

Vicky leaned forward conspiratorially. 'Over there is a *fully* qualified veterinary surgeon.'

The farmer followed her pointing finger, but could only see Jenny leaning over the horse's leg.

'Where?' he said. Then he realised who Vicky meant. 'You mean . . . ?'

'Yes,' said Vicky, 'and she's straight from England. She'd be one of the best in the colonies. She's got letters after her name.'

Those words had the desired effect. The way the farmer reacted, you would've thought they were pure gold. He thanked Vicky profusely and swaggered across the street to talk to Jenny. 'Well,' he muttered to himself, 'who'd've thought. A woman vet'inary . . . still, I'll not be one to look a gift horse in the mouth.'

Vicky chuckled happily and went inside the shop. 'Shop,' she cried, seeing no-one in the place.

This time it was Hilda Burton who appeared from beneath the counter.

'Oh, it's you!' Mrs Burton was surprised. But she didn't look displeased, either. In fact, although Hilda Burton was as tough as the iron she fashioned to her will, she was equally loyal to people she took a shine to. She didn't suffer fools, but if she liked you, she would help you to the bitter end.

She had thought that Vicky and Jenny would take one look at the farm and be on the next boat back to England. Obviously, they weren't going to let it affect them. Hilda Burton had a strong feeling that she was going to like these new arrivals.

'Well, what can I do for you?' she asked.

'I've got a list of the extra goods we need,' Vicky said brightly. She noticed Mr Burton entering the shop. 'You'll be pleased to know we're staying.'

'Oh, that *is* nice,' Mrs Burton said. 'Isn't it, dear?'

Samuel Burton just grunted. 'I'll attend to their supplies.' He went about the shop, grabbing a tin of this here and a packet of that there, muttering sourly to himself. Hilda returned her attention to Vicky.

'So, how's your mother? Is she here?'

'She's my step-mother. She's outside,' Vicky cast a sidelong glance at Mr Burton and raised her voice a fraction. 'She's a fully qualified veterinary surgeon.'

Mr Burton almost dropped what he was carrying. Vicky tried hard not to laugh – and Hilda, who could see exactly what Vicky had done, couldn't resist smiling herself. She reached into one of the glass jars on the counter, pulled out a large gobstopper and popped it into Vicky's mouth. She put a silent finger to her lips – 'don't tell Samuel,' it said.

Vicky's mouth was just able to close itself around the sweet as Samuel Burton turned around. 'Was it *four* bars of soap you wanted?'

Vicky couldn't open her mouth to speak. She just nodded her head – Mr Burton glared at her

82

and returned to his work, mumbling about 'how rude young girls were these days'. Hilda and Vicky revelled in their private joke.

Meanwhile, Jenny had seen to Constable Carmody's horse and was now examining the ailing calf.

'Looks like lead poisoning,' she pronounced after checking inside the animal's mouth and massaging its heaving stomach. 'Don't ever have paintwork in the barn. The animals lick it and something like this happens.'

'Well now, can you do something about it? That's what I have to know . . . '

'I'll be out this afternoon with some magnesium sulphate. That should fix them up quickly enough.'

The farmer looked like he was happy enough to burst. Suddenly all the worries of the world had been lifted from his shoulders. He took Jenny's hand, shaking it up and down like he was priming a water pump.

'Thank you, ma'am. Thank you again. I'll be sure and tell the other farmers around about, don't you worry 'bout that.'

'I'll see you this afternoon then,' Jenny said, suddenly keen to check up on Vicky's progress. The farmer nodded vigorously, jumped into his cart and took off along the track.

Jenny couldn't believe it. The problem with the farmer's animals had been so easily solved, but what had worried her were the tales of an untrained veterinarian who had been feeding the local farmers a lot of harmful old wives' tales. There was clearly going to be a lot for her to do.

She joined Vicky at the shop counter.

'It's criminal you know,' she said loudly. 'There's some quack around here calling himself a veterinarian. He's doing all sorts of damage to the livestock in the district. Honestly, there ought to be a law against . . . '

Vicky, her mouth still firmly filled with the gob-stopper, hadn't been able to stop Jenny's outburst. She grabbed Jenny's arm and pointed towards Mr Burton. He was standing on a small stepladder, where he'd been retrieving some stock. Now he stood there quivering with rage. None of this made any sense at all to Jenny, until she saw a sign hanging over the counter, 'Consulting Veterinary'.

'Oh!' Jenny choked on the rest of her sentence, 'I see.'

Burton continued making up the order, but was pointedly sulking at Jenny's attack on his credibility.

'Ah . . . is there anything else we need, Vicky?' Jenny wanted to get out of there as quickly as possible. Vicky shook her head, still unable to speak.

Like Burton, Jenny could only guess that Vicky was being rude. 'What's the matter? Cat got your tongue?'

Vicky shook her head.

12

Manfred was doing what he loved best. He had dismantled the flying machine and was now recoating its canvas wings with a specially prepared resin to impart greater strength and to enable it to 'hold the wind' more easily.

It was such a glorious, sunny day that he had brought Black Beauty out and tethered him nearby. No animal deserved to be cooped up in a dark barn with the weather like this.

He had laid the wings across three trestles, and was painting the resin on from all sides. Occasionally the wind came up – and this showed how aerodynamically sound his design was – it could sometimes lift the wings right off the trestle. Then it would take all Manfred's considerable strength to keep them from launching into the air.

Suddenly, though, the wind changed. An unexpectedly strong gust blew the wings up and away before Manfred could drag them back down. He gave chase as the wings tumbled about, straight for Black Beauty. The stallion reared up, pulling at the tethered cord.

'Hey . . . whoa boy. It's all right. These wings, they will not hurt you.'

But it was too late. Beauty jerked his strong head back and the cord snapped. He dodged the wings and swerved away, across the field and over a nearby fence. Manfred raced after him in vain, as Beauty galloped powerfully back into the hills from where he came.

Manfred watched, horrified, and sank to his knees. How could he tell Miss Vicky?

Half-way home, Vicky finally swallowed her gobstopper.

'I can talk again now,' she announced.

'I should probably keep a bag of those things handy,' Jenny said slyly. 'I'm sure they would be useful . . .'

'Very funny. What's that stuff you said you'd give to the cows?'

'Magnesium sulphate?'

'Mmm. What's that?'

'Nothing much – it's more commonly known as Epsom Salts.'

Well now, that *was* funny, Vicky thought. Cunning too. It showed Jenny was sharp enough to survive out here where it really was a man's world. Suddenly, Vicky felt a lot better about their prospects.

All of a sudden, though, their quiet ride home was brought to a standstill. Frank Coates was blocking the track on his horse, waiting for them.

'G'day ladies,' he said, very polite but clearly not meaning a word of it. 'How do you do?'

He lifted his hat with something of a flourish. Jenny smiled. At least this man had a bit of character, which was more than she'd seen from the locals so far.

'Good morning. I'm Mrs Denning and this is my step-daughter Victoria.'

'Frank Coates. I live about six miles up the road from you.' He paused deliberately for effect. 'I run horses.'

'That's a happy coincidence, Mr Coates. I'm a veterinary surgeon and I specialise in horses.'

'Well, blow me down. A woman veterinary.'

'Yes,' Jenny stiffened slightly. 'I suppose I am that – a woman veterinary. There are more of us every day, you know.'

'I'm sure there are.' Coates turned to Vicky. 'Do you like horses, young lady?'

'Yes I do.'

'So do I.' He grinned broadly, as if laughing at his own private joke. 'I'll be seeing you, I expect.'

'I hope to be seeing you, Mr Coates,' Jenny answered, but Coates was already a good distance away and he didn't look back. Jenny looked at Vicky and shrugged.

'He must be new,' Vicky said. 'A lot of people have moved in since we went away.'

They continued towards home, discussing plans for the future and the immediate problems in fixing up the farm. As they neared the entrance, Manfred walked out to meet them. The haunted expression on his face said it all.

'Beauty!!' Vicky broke into a gallop, and rushed to the barn. 'Beauty!!' He wasn't there. Then she saw the broken fence – she turned to face Manfred. 'Where is he?'

'He went very fast. I try to catch him but he smashed through the fence. I did not see him again.'

Jenny looked around at the tattered remains of Manfred's machine and immediately realised what had happened. 'He's half wild, Manfred,' she admonished. 'The slightest thing will scare him.'

Vicky rounded on him. 'You should've been more careful!'

Manfred agreed, ashamed at failing to help his new friends. What could he do?. He would do anything to try and make things right.

Jenny tried to console Vicky. 'He is wild. You knew there was every chance something like this could happen.'

'We have to go after him – now!'

'We can't.'

'Why not?' Vicky shouted. Jenny looked at her. She wasn't going to stand for this sort of nonsense.

'Manfred, take the horses into the barn please.' Then she noticed his clothes, filthy from chasing and diving after Beauty. 'And you might like to clean yourself up.'

Ignoring Vicky, she strode on into the house. Vicky was stunned at this treatment. She followed close on Jenny's heels.

Vicky found Jenny in the kitchen, packing her veterinary bag.

'If he's running,' she pleaded, 'he might snag himself on that rope.'

'He'll stop running soon enough,' Jenny replied tersely, 'and he's well able to look after himself.'

'Jenny, we've got to go and look for him now. Please.'

'No. I have to make that call now.' Jenny was becoming really irritated.

'Just one hour . . .'

'One hour longer and those calves will be suffering even more badly. They may die and then the farmer will have lost his livelihood. If I let him down, we're finished before we start. Our livelihood depends on this, too. Surely you can see that?'

But Vicky couldn't see anything of the sort. Her mind was closed to everything except Black Beauty, and she couldn't believe that Jenny, of all people, would stop her saving him from danger.

'I will go by myself.'

'You will not. If you don't find him, you'll be out all night.'

'I'll take Manfred, then.'

For Jenny, that was the final straw. She stormed around the kitchen table and pushed Vicky down on to the seat. 'Manfred cannot ride. Now I am going out – I'll be back before dark. Are you listening to me? You will not go looking for Black Beauty alone!'

But there was no reaction from Vicky. She was wilful and stubborn, everything her father and grand-father had always said. Jenny had often been accused of the same things. Now she was on the receiving end, and she was furious, but tired of arguing.

'You will not go looking for Black Beauty alone. Is that understood?'

There was nothing else for Vicky to do. She gave a very slight, barely perceptible, nod of her head. But it was enough. 'Good,' said Jenny, sweeping off out the door. 'I won't be long.'

Vicky was inconsolable. But she wasn't the kind of girl to give up easily – pretty soon, she had to do something. She had to take action.

She went to the barn to confront Manfred. He apologised immediately for his part in Beauty's breaking out and, even though he was obviously very upset, Vicky still couldn't forgive him.

'If my flying machine was ready, I could find him very quickly.' Manfred was trying to make her feel better, but it didn't work. In fact, quite the opposite – it made her feel that Manfred was stupid. Stupid for letting Black Beauty escape and stupid for wasting his time trying to fly when he couldn't even ride a horse.

She glared at him angrily. 'Well it's not ready. It may never be ready – I don't care about your silly flying machine. I want to find my horse.'

She shouldn't have said it. She knew that, and see-ing Manfred's pained reaction made her feel guilty. He looked shattered, as if someone had told him his best friend had died. Vicky knew what that felt like.

'I'm sorry,' she relented. 'I just want to be out looking for him. Why can't you ride, Manfred? Then we could go searching together.'

Manfred told her his secret. 'I have tried. But every time I ride a horse, the horse tells me to get off. So, instead, I ride this . . . '

He pointed towards the far wall, where a trusty two-wheeled bicycle stood, waiting to go.

'Manfred! You've got a bike.' For some reason, Vicky seemed very excited. Manfred couldn't understand it.

'Yes . . . ' he said slowly. 'But I don't see . . . '

'Now I won't have to go alone,' Vicky cried. 'It'll be all right. Come on, I'll saddle up. We can be gone in five minutes.'

'I don't think Mrs Denning would . . . ' Manfred began to protest before Vicky cut him off again.

'She said I wasn't to go alone. Well, I'm not alone now, so it's all right for us to start looking. Hurry up, Manfred.'

Now that Vicky had found a way around Jenny's order not to go, she leapt at it. Before Manfred even had time to think, she had saddled up her horse and dragged the bicycle outside. She knew they had to get moving, there were only a few hours before sunset. After that, it might be too late.

She took off across the field, setting a tough pace for poor old Manfred, struggling on his bike.

'Which way did he go?' Vicky turned to see Manfred huffing and puffing behind her. 'Come on! You'll have to go faster than that if we're to get anywhere tonight . . . '

Manfred took the conversation as an excuse to stop and get his breath back. He pointed straight ahead. 'He go over the hill.'

'That's very wild country,' Vicky wondered aloud. 'It's steep and the footing is treacherous for horses.'

Manfred tried to allay her fears. 'There are new farms now, since you've been away. It's not so wild, I think.'

Vicky looked up at the rapidly darkening sky and hesitated. Manfred noticed. 'Shall we leave this? Try again tomorrow, with more help, yes?'

But Vicky was definite. 'No,' she said firmly, leaving no room for doubt. 'We're going on . . . '

After a while they came to the end of the trail that Manfred had seen Black Beauty take. From here, it would be guesswork. Vicky tried to put herself in Beauty's place – where would he go? Two distinct choices presented themselves. First, he could have gone inland, downhill into the bush country with plenty of food and cover. That was the most obvious route. The other was to veer left towards the coast and its hard, flat beaches. A rogue stallion would be an easy target there, but Vicky just had a feeling . . .

'This way, Manfred,' she called out to her lagging companion, pointing towards the bay. Manfred looked surprised at her sudden change in direction. It was just a hunch, but she could feel Beauty drawn towards the freedom of the coastal flatlands and the exhilarating, pounding surf. He had been kept against his will and badly treated. Vicky knew she was right – he would head for the sea.

They took the most direct route to the coast, keeping to a prominent ridge until the ground fell away sharply, revealing the breakers smashing on to the rocks below.

Vicky circled around, trying to find a safe way down. At one point the earth gave way, sending a shower of gravel over the edge. Vicky's horse whinnied in alarm. Its cry was echoed by another, coming from below.

Vicky quickly dismounted and threw her head over the edge of the cliff. Her heart sank. Black Beauty was balanced delicately on a narrow ledge about five metres down. Vicky could see where he had fallen, sliding to a halt just before a sheer drop which would have killed him. Worse still, his leading rope had become snagged between two rocks.

'Take it easy Beauty, don't move . . . I'm here. I'll help you.' Vicky spoke quietly, reassuring her friend.

As she talked, she drew herself out over the cliff and began edging tentatively towards him. She was half-way down when Manfred peered over the top of the precipice. Seeing her horse tied up alone, he had feared the worst. Now, he looked on as Vicky quickly sized up the danger – Vicky was risking her life going down there without ropes.

'What are you doing? We must go back for help!' he yelled.

'There isn't time. Beauty will die if we don't bring him up before nightfall.' Vicky hadn't taken her eyes off the horse. She held out her hand. 'It's all right, Beauty, don't move. I'm not going to hurt you. We're friends, remember?'

The slope down wasn't as steep as it looked. But loose gravel on top made the going slippery. Fine showers of tiny stones fell away from her feet at each step and careered down the hill towards Beauty. The stallion moved about nervously, making high-pitched neighing sounds.

'Steady boy . . . steady.' Then Vicky was at his side. She pulled at his rope, but couldn't free it. 'Have you got a knife or something,' she called out to Manfred.

Manfred searched frantically through his pockets and found a penknife deep in his back trouser pocket. He started to come down the cliff-face himself, but Vicky motioned him back.

'No! Just slide it. Slide it to me.' She didn't stop stroking Beauty's mane. 'It's all right boy. We'll get you free in no time . . .'

Manfred took aim and let go of the knife. It skidded down the slope, just out of Vicky's reach, and ended up balanced on the edge of a sheer drop. Vicky let go of Beauty and moved towards it, step by agonising step. She drew level with it but, leaning forward, it was still just out of reach.

She lay down and slowly crawled ahead an inch at a time, trying not to overbalance. As Manfred watched anxiously, her hand closed around the knife handle and she was able to drag herself a safe distance away before standing up again.

Now, the trick was to get close enough to Beauty before cutting the rope so he wouldn't startle and fall. Ever so carefully, Vicky cut at the lead – once, twice, then on the third strike the last strand gave way. Beauty was free. He skittered a little now that the tight rein no longer held him back.

'Easy, my Beauty . . . come on, you can back up now. Back up.' Vicky could see it wouldn't be easy going back the way they came down. She led Beauty around the cliff until they reached a point where the incline was not so steep. Then, straining as they went, they pulled each other to the top until once again they were on safe ground.

Then Vicky did a strange thing. She took the rest of Beauty's rope off from around his head. Manfred couldn't understand it.

'You will need the rope to lead him,' he reminded Vicky.

'Beauty doesn't want to be led. I tried to tame him, Manfred, and he broke loose . . . I nearly killed him.'

93

'But that was my fault,' Manfred declared. 'That is no reason for you to let him go now that he is safe.'

'If Beauty wants to come back to us, he will. The decision must be his, not ours.' Vicky stroked the horse's neck one final time, then turned and mounted her mare. She rode off over the hill without another backward glance. Manfred stood dismayed, but there was nothing he could do. He picked up his bike and followed Vicky back to the house.

Black Beauty let them go. He made no move.

Vicky didn't stop until she was outside their own front door. All the time, she had listened in vain for the sound of Beauty's hooves behind her. But the sound never came.

She got off her horse and sat, despondent, on the verandah. A short time later, Manfred rode up the path and came alongside her. He placed a consoling hand on her shoulder. To Vicky, however, it felt like the heavy hand of defeat because she knew now that she had lost the one thing in the world that really mattered to her. She tried hard to feel happy for the beautiful black horse which was now running free.

'Manfred, do you think I did the right thing?'

Manfred didn't reply. What could he say? He turned away, unsure how to react. All of a sudden, he pulled her around so that she was standing in front of him. His hands covered her eyes so she couldn't see a thing.

'Yes,' he whispered into her ear. 'Yes, Vicky, you did the right thing.' His hands pulled away and the darkness lifted. She was looking into the sun. Vicky blinked twice, trying to adjust to the light, but something was moving in the distance in front of her.

Vicky felt her heart leap to her throat. For a moment, she couldn't speak, she could hardly even move, she was so overcome with joy. Black Beauty was galloping free across the field towards her. It was possibly the best moment in Vicky's life.

Beauty slowed down as Vicky raced out to greet him. He bent his head forward for her embrace and whinnied softly as she talked to him.

'I knew you'd follow, Beauty. I knew you would. You're not wild, you're just scared of people, aren't you?' Then with sudden certainty, she turned to Manfred. 'Get the saddle, please.'

Manfred's eyebrows arched up in surprise. 'What? I don't think I should.'

But Vicky was firm. 'I'm going to saddle Black Beauty.'

'He's not ready. Jenny says so. She knows – so do you. Look what happened today, Beauty gets scared at the smallest thing.'

Vicky ran her hand through Beauty's mane again. The horse snorted in pleasure. 'No he doesn't. He just needs to know he's with a friend, that's all. Isn't it, Beauty?'

Manfred shrugged and began unbuckling the saddle from the mare Vicky had ridden before. He wasn't as sure about this as Vicky but, then again, he didn't know anything about horses and he certainly wasn't a match for Vicky when she wanted her way. I may as well help her, he thought. Otherwise she will just go off and do it herself – at least, this way I'm here to help if anything goes wrong.

'Vicky, I do not like this.' Manfred watched as the girl made final adjustments to Beauty's saddle. The stallion was becoming skittish, moving about nervously.

'Somebody has tried to saddle him before – and used a whip to keep in the saddle,' Vicky replied, confidently. 'I won't use a whip.'

'He does not know that,' Manfred pointed out.

'He will. And when he does, he'll trust me. Won't you, my Beauty?'

'But he is not tame.'

Vicky sighed. Poor Manfred, he didn't understand and he never would. He was so clever with machines but the beauty of animals escaped him completely. 'I don't want a tame horse, Manfred. I want one that's alive, with a mind of its own.' She gave Beauty a friendly pat on his flank. 'Ready, boy?'

She placed her foot in the stirrup and pulled herself up into the saddle. Beauty reared sharply and Vicky tumbled on to the ground on the other side. But she was up again in a trice, dusting herself off, not in the least worried. Not like Manfred, who was biting his fingernails as he watched.

'I won't hurt you,' Vicky whispered, encouragingly. Up she got again, with the same result. This time, Vicky landed face down in the mud, her riding dress ruined. But it only made her more determined than ever. She patted Black Beauty's muzzle and, the moment he stood still, she remounted him.

This time, Beauty bucked hard but Vicky managed to hang on. She leaned forward, stroking his mane. Gradually, she realised that this time Beauty had accepted her. She looked over at Manfred in triumph. He had noticed it too, and smiled broadly back at her.

'I think he likes you.'

'We are going to be very, very good friends. I can feel it.'

She raised her head to Manfred again, but something behind him caused her smile to fade. Manfred turned to see that Jenny had returned – and she looked very angry indeed.

Vicky got down from her horse. She felt scared. She had never seen Jenny look like this.

Jenny spoke first. 'I think an explanation is in order.'

Vicky started to say something, but Jenny cut in sharply. 'In the house,' she snapped, and strode inside herself without waiting for Vicky to follow.

Manfred felt sorry for Vicky as she trod reluctantly into the house. He knew how much she had wanted to find Beauty, and he'd seen how bravely she had rescued the magnificent black stallion from that ledge. But in the mood that Jenny was in, she wouldn't want to listen to any excuses – and it wasn't Manfred's place to intervene in a family dispute. He stayed outside, hoping Jenny would not be too hard on her step-daughter.

Although the other two did not realise it, Jenny was more scared than angry. Vicky had disobeyed her – not only had she gone out searching for her missing horse, but she had tried riding him when Jenny had specifically ordered her not to.

But that was not what worried Jenny. The fact that Vicky had gone off on her own, without telling her, really frightened Jenny. It was time for them to sort things out once and for all.

'This is a strange land for me,' Jenny started off saying, once Vicky was inside. 'If you hadn't come back, I wouldn't have known where to start looking for you.'

Vicky said nothing, so Jenny continued: 'There are going to be more days like this, when I am away from this house. I have to know I can trust you.'

'I know it was wrong,' Vicky was nearly crying. She had to make Jenny understand. 'But I wanted to find Beauty more than anything.'

'That's not good enough. I'm responsible for you. And I care about you. Would you have done this to your father? What if he'd come back and found you missing?'

Vicky had not thought of it like this. And Jenny mentioning her father made her think and hope for his safe return all over again.

'Do you think he will come back?' she asked, falling into Jenny's waiting arms.

'Oh, Vicky, I don't know. I really don't . . . but if he does, I want him to find us together. I want him to come home to a family.'

Vicky thought about what Jenny had said. 'I'm sorry,' she said finally. 'I won't disobey you again.'

Jenny smiled. 'I know you won't.' They hugged each other tight. But their embrace was cut short by the sound of someone outside. They ran to the door.

A man was approaching on horseback up the path. Manfred left his machinery to welcome their guest – Frank Coates, the man who had met them on their way home from town, and who had secretly watched them from a far hilltop.

Jenny and Vicky stood on the verandah. 'Maybe he needs some veterinary help,' Jenny said. Vicky wasn't so sure. She didn't really trust this man – he had a smiling face, but his eyes never smiled.

Mr Coates touched his wide-brimmed hat in greeting. 'G'day,' he said jovially. 'It's Frank Coates . . . '

Jenny was friendly in return. 'I remember you, Mr Coates. How can I be of help?'

Coates grinned. 'Oh, easy enough. You can give me back my horse.'

'What?' Jenny and Vicky said at once.

Coates turned and pointed at Black Beauty. 'The black one in your paddock.'

'No, he's ours,' Vicky cried.

'He's mine and I want him back,' Coates hadn't stopped grinning, but his smile was forced and his lips had drawn tight over his teeth. He did not look friendly.

'No!' Vicky ran down the verandah steps and climbed the fence to reach Beauty.

'Have you any proof?' Jenny stepped in, not liking the look of this one little bit.

'I certainly do,' Coates replied harshly. 'He's mine. He's mine and I'll have him back . . . '

'No! You can't have him!' Vicky clung on to Beauty's neck as if for dear life.

Now Manfred stepped forward, ready to take Coates on if need be. Coates sized him up. 'Why, you young whippersnapper. I'll . . . '

But Jenny stopped him in mid-sentence. '*I'm* not a young whippersnapper, Mr Coates, and I suggest you leave here before there's any trouble. I don't think it would look too good for you if we had you arrested for trespass, would it?'

Coates thought for a minute and gave a grudging nod. He wheeled his horse around and galloped down the path, through the Denning farm gate.

Outside their property, he turned and yelled to them. 'Don't think you've seen the last of me yet. I'll be back – back to claim what's mine . . . '

13

The next morning, they had another visitor. This time he really *was* a whippersnapper. A boy – he wouldn't have been more than seven or eight years old – ran around the house, looking for something.

Vicky was in the barn with Beauty. She did not want him out of her sight after the scare with Mr Coates the previous night. They were nuzzled up close together, so she didn't hear the boy as he moved about their property in his barefeet.

He did not seem to know where to go or what he was supposed to do. Finally, he knocked on the back door. Manfred answered, eating his toast. The boy was quite out of breath. It took him quite some time before he was able to speak.

'Is this where the new animal doctor lives?' he gasped.

Jenny appeared from the hallway. 'That's me . . . do you need some help?'

The boy looked startled. 'But you're a *lady*, ma'am,' he said, as if that settled the matter – she couldn't possibly be a vet.

'I *am* the vet,' Jenny said firmly. 'What can I do for you?'

The boy thought it over. It was obvious he needed help, so if this woman said she was the vet, it wasn't up to him to argue. 'Me dad wants you. Our pig's having little'uns. But she won't. She keeps going . . .'

Then the boy went into a great spasm, rolling around the kitchen floor, clutching his stomach and groaning realistically.

'Goodness,' said Jenny, reaching for her bag. 'She *does* need help. Where is your farm?'

'Eight miles,' the boy said, proudly pointing to the northern road. 'I runned all the way.'

Jenny and Manfred smiled. The little boy looked extremely serious, and he had done his job very well. Manfred went over to him and shook his hand. 'Very well done, young sir,' he said. 'Now, do you think you will show us how to get back to your place?'

'Yes. Yes, I will,' the boy nodded vigorously.

Manfred turned to Jenny. 'I will harness the trap?'

'Yes, and tell Vicky where I'm going. I don't want her galavanting off somewhere while I'm away.'

In the barn, Manfred gave her the message. Vicky was not the only one worried about Coates, Manfred was trying to figure it out as well. 'There are many wild horses in this part of New Zealand, Vicky. Why does Coates think he owns this one?'

'Because he knows how good Beauty is. He was just trying to bully us.'

Manfred considered this. 'Mr Coates is a hard man. But he is not a thief,' he said. Then he smiled. 'He was very angry when Mrs Denning told him to go . . .'

Vicky nodded, but could not laugh about it like Manfred. She was deep in thought when Jenny entered the barn with the little boy who was now munching hungrily on a piece of homemade bread.

'Come on, up you hop, young lad.' Jenny beamed at Vicky and Manfred. 'My second customer, things are looking up.'

'Jenny,' Vicky said, changing the subject, 'why does Mr Coates think Beauty belongs to him?'

Jenny thought but could not find an answer. 'I don't know but don't worry, we'll sort it out.'

'What if he comes back?'

'Then we'll give him the runaround like we did yesterday. You just forget about it. There are plenty of chores to do round here that will take your mind off it. I'll be back as soon as I can.'

Jenny took hold of the reins and guided the trap out through the double barn doors. Vicky waved goodbye, but her mind was preoccupied. She brought Black Beauty out into the fresh air and into a paddock to graze.

'Beauty belongs here,' she said fiercely. 'We belong here together.'

'Not if I can help it,' a voice jarred her to her senses. Behind her sat three men on horseback – Mr Coates, flanked by his foreman Lewis Duncan and Constable Carmody.

Vicky could see that this time Mr Coates meant business. She flew to Beauty's side. 'No,' she shouted. 'Go away.'

'He has the right, missy,' Constable Carmody stated flatly.

'He can't have. I don't believe you,' Vicky responded. Her cries brought Manfred running over.

'What is happening here?'

'I was just explaining to the young lady,' Constable Carmody said, 'Mr Coates has rights to catch wild horses in this district. The horse here is his.'

Coates got down from his own horse, a chestnut mare of good breeding. 'You stopped me last night, but today I've got the law on my side.'

'But constable, he didn't catch this one,' Vicky pleaded. 'We did.'

'That's right,' Manfred chipped in. 'He's at home here.'

'Home,' Coates sneered. 'The only home he's got is in my stables. He was there for a long time, and he got away. You just ask my foreman.'

All eyes turned to Lewis Duncan. He was a handsome fellow, in a roguish sort of way, in his early twenties – rough but intelligent, and good with horses.

Lewis blinked. He felt uncomfortable with everyone staring at him. But he looked over at the black stallion, grazing in the field, and nodded in agreement. 'That's him all right.'

'How can you tell?' Vicky demanded. 'By those rope marks?'

'I didn't do that,' Lewis said quickly. And he meant it. He would *never* mistreat a horse like that, but there were others he had no power over who did not feel the same way.

Men like Coates. 'He's my horse,' he growled. 'Leave him to me.'

Vicky tried to block his way. 'Now, miss,' Constable Carmody warned, 'I'd rather no laws were broken . . . because then I might have to arrest someone. I don't think your mother would approve of that.'

'But you just can't let him take Beauty,' Vicky said. Beauty, however, had no intention of going anywhere with Coates. He reared up violently – Coates got out of the way just in time, falling backwards head-over-heels. Lewis put his hand over his mouth, hiding a grin. Even Constable Carmody's normally serious face flickered in good humour at the sight.

Coates, of course, was furious. 'I'll teach you . . . ' He drew out a whip from a holder in his saddle. 'Don't you dare hit him!' Vicky yelled and rushed forward, grabbing his arm. They struggled until Constable Carmody's sharp voice put a stop to it.

'All right, that's enough, Mr Coates. You've got your horse, now I suggest you leave quietly.' He was in no mood for argument. Even an ill-tempered Coates saw no reason to tangle with the law. He signalled to Lewis to tie Black Beauty to his horse.

'He's not your horse, Mr Coates, and he never will be,' Vicky said, challenging him.

The men ignored her and turned to go. 'I won't let you keep him,' she added angrily. But the men weren't listening. There was nothing she could do. Vicky fell to the ground and began to cry.

Jenny couldn't believe it. 'They just came back on to the farm?' she asked, incredulous, as Manfred spilled out the news. 'We'll see about that. Where's Vicky now?'

'In the house,' Manfred said. 'She is very angry.'

'So am I,' Jenny replied. 'So am I.'

She found Vicky in her bedroom, her bed strewn with jewellery given to her by Lord Fordham. Jenny knocked and entered. 'Are you planning on buying him back?'

'If I have to, I will,' Vicky said, sounding determined. 'I'll give Mr Coates the brooch and this gold necklace . . .'

'Vicky, those are heirlooms. They're worth twenty times the value of a horse.'

'I'd give them all for Beauty,' said Vicky, looking as if she was about to cry all over again. She took a deep breath and the feeling passed. The time for crying, she told herself, was over. Beauty needed her, and she would do whatever was necessary to get him back.

'I know you would,' Jenny said, taking Vicky's arm. 'But I've thought of a better way. Come with me.'

It was Jenny's opinion that nothing ever got done by worrying about it. You had to strike, she said, at the heart of the problem. So she took Vicky straight to the Coates' farm.

Coates hadn't wasted any time. He and his men were already at work on Beauty, trying to break him in. But they hadn't even managed to get the saddle over his back. Beauty was rearing his forelegs and bucking his hind legs, and generally making a terrible fuss.

'Come on, lads,' Coates was yelling. 'Get that saddle strap on tight.' Again they tried, and again Black Beauty reared up, whinnying impressively as if to say, 'You will never tame me.'

The men scattered and Coates, who had been holding the leading rope on Beauty's head, lost his footing completely and sprawled headlong in the mud. He got to his feet to see Jenny and Vicky doing their best not to laugh at him.

'No need to stand on my account, Mr Coates,' Jenny said, slyly.

Coates scowled. 'I know why you're here. Well you're out of luck – he's not for sale.'

Vicky reached into her pocket and was about to say something, when Jenny held her back. She indicated across the field with a nod of her head. 'That mare will be foaling in due course. I expect it's her first?'

Coates nodded grumpily, 'Yeah, so what?'

'From the look of those hips, she'll have trouble.'

Coates laughed. 'I see your game. Well, it won't work. You're not the only veterinary around here . . . '

'I am for twenty miles. What about that one,' she added, pointing to another horse. 'He's favouring a foreleg. You're wasting your time trying to break him. And as for that black and white two year old . . . '

'What's wrong with him?' Coates snapped.

'If you want to know that, then you'll have to take me on as your vet,' Jenny answered cleverly.

Coates considered this for a while, but would not give in. 'I was in the West Australian Light Horse Brigade. I know about horses.'

'You still need a good vet.' Then Jenny made her offer. 'I'll give you my services for six months – in exchange for Black Beauty.'

Vicky chipped in, holding out her brooch. 'And I'll give you this.'

Coates winced. He was clearly embarrassed by this show of affection for a horse that he wanted solely because it would fetch a good price. 'I don't want your baubles,' he said roughly. 'The horse is not for sale.'

'You'll never ride him,' Vicky replied, goading him a little.

'Yes, I will. There's not a horse been born that I can't ride.'

Vicky pointed across at Black Beauty, alone in the riding ring. The men didn't want to get too close for fear of losing their teeth to a well aimed kick. 'You can't even get the saddle on,' she laughed.

And before anyone could say a word, Vicky slipped down from the trap and walked right up to Beauty. Beauty quivered and give her a little 'hello' snort. 'It's all right, my Beauty . . . all right.'

Lewis and the other men watched, impressed, as Vicky slipped the saddle across Beauty's back and tightened the strap. Beauty did not even flinch. Vicky turned and eyed Coates defiantly. 'See,' she told him.

Then, with a quick movement, she mounted Black Beauty and rode him around the inside of the ring – close to the fence so that the men had to scamper over it to get out of the way.

Lewis and the rest of the stablehands were astonished at Vicky's performance. She looked at them, then at Coates. 'You don't like Black Beauty, because he won't let you ride him. Beauty knows that . . . he's been treated harshly, so you have to take time to earn his trust.'

Coates whacked his hat against his leg in disgust. 'Ah, one horse doesn't make any difference. My Dancer there could run the legs off him.'

Vicky was immediately interested. 'All right then, let's try it. Black Beauty against Dancer.'

'Vicky . . . ' Jenny's voice was warning her off.

Coates, however, was seriously considering Vicky's offer. He looked at her and laughed. 'I've been on horseback before you were born. It wouldn't be a fair match.'

Vicky shook her head. 'You give me one week with Black Beauty. Then we'll race over a measured course.'

'A week?' Coates asked. Vicky nodded.

'Winner take all?' Again, Vicky nodded her agreement.

'Winner take all,' she repeated. 'We'll start on the beach, run up the river, through town and Miller's Gorge, and end up back at the beach.'

Hearing this, Coates tried to hide his smile. Beside him, Bert grinned mischievously and Lewis looked a little worried. But Vicky did not notice – she was happy to have Black Beauty back, and glad for the slim chance she had to keep him.

Jenny noticed the men's reaction, though. And it troubled her.

Coates opened the riding pen gate with a flourish to let Vicky and Beauty out.

'You've got yourself a race, young lady,' he declared. 'Seven days from today. You can have the horse till then.'

Vicky rode Beauty through the gate, and tied his halter rope to the trap.

'Good luck, Missy . . . eh lads?'

The stablemen laughed, all except for Lewis. Jenny flicked the reins, and the horse and trap slowly left the Coates' farm, with Beauty pacing leisurely behind.

Vicky was smiling uncontrollably. But, once they were out of earshot, Jenny turned to her and said, very seriously, 'Remember, he's not yours yet.'

'Oh, I can beat him over that course,' Vicky said casually. 'I've ridden over it hundreds of times.'

'That was two years ago, Vicky. Let's go and have a look at it after lunch, shall we?'

'Why?' Vicky asked. She couldn't understand why Jenny was so serious after she had so brilliantly persuaded Coates to let her have Black Beauty back.

'Because,' Jenny said, sounding worried, 'Mr Coates looked far too happy.'

14

Constable Carmody emerged out of Burton's shop with a bag of boiled sweets in his hand and a large gobstopper rolling around in his mouth.

Looking up, he saw Jenny and Vicky riding into town. Vicky, he was astonished to note, rode in on Black Beauty – after all the trouble he'd gone to making sure it went back to Mr Coates!

'Good afternoon, Constable Carmody,' Jenny smiled. 'And how is your horse today?'

'He's well, very well, Mrs Denning,' Constable Carmody replied. 'And I see you have the horse you wanted, Miss Vicky. Might I ask how you come to be riding him?'

'We came to an arrangement with Mr Coates,' Jenny answered for Vicky, then quickly changed the subject. 'By the way, have you found out what happened to our stock?'

'Ah . . . no. But I'm getting on to it,' the constable said with a practised frown showing on his face. He was always serious when it came to his work.

Vicky, meanwhile, was busy reading a sign displayed in Burton's shop window. Mr Burton peered out from behind the sign, then disappeared. Surprise, surprise . . . he soon came bustling out of the shop, pretending to examine his stock on the front verandah. He was just being his normal, inquisitive self.

Vicky spoke up, 'Mr Burton, you're advertising for a postie. I'd like to apply for the job.'

Vicky's request caught Burton quite off balance. He spluttered a little, then puffed himself up with self-importance. 'Ah . . . as the regional postmaster, I . . . I suppose I could consider it.'

'Thank you, Mr Burton,' Vicky said brightly.

'Good day, gentlemen,' Jenny said, just as brightly. And the Dennings rode off happily down the main street, leaving the two men on Burton's verandah wondering if they were the subjects of some kind of women's joke.

Really, Jenny and Vicky were just very happy – although for different reasons. Vicky, of course, had Black Beauty and the prospect of her race in a week's time to look forward to.

But it was Jenny who had gone through the greatest change. She had arrived in this strange place only weeks ago, in the very worst of circumstances, but now felt much more settled and content.

She was beginning to get veterinary work. Despite their surprise at a woman doing the job, these farmers were impressed with her knowledge and were smart enough to know when they might be on to a good thing. Yes, Jenny felt, it might be possible to settle down here, after all.

However, this happy couple weren't so cheerful when it came time to inspect the racecourse that Vicky had so confidently proposed.

It was just as Jenny had feared. She and Vicky found the river and headed inland from the beach. They followed it, Vicky leading the way.

'It's a clean gallop from here to town,' Vicky was saying, but her voice tailed off as they rounded a bend in the shallow river. Instead of the easy slopes, native bush and riding trails of her earlier days in Puhoi, Vicky was faced with what looked like a battle zone.

The hillside was muddy and eroded. The bush and trees were all gone – only broken tree stumps and a litter of fallen timber suggested this had once been a pleasant place to ride.

'It's not what I'd call a clean gallop,' Jenny declared. 'It hardly safe enough to walk through, let alone ride.'

'But it's changed. How was I to know? It's not the way it was before.'

Suddenly, there was a rustle of dead leaves at the top of the hill. Lewis appeared and slid down the slope to meet them.

'G'dday,' he said, seeming quite friendly without Mr Coates around. 'It was the timber company. It moved in up the top there last year. They cut down all the standing trees – too many of them, the fools – and the rain did the rest. Nobody uses this track now, I'm afraid.'

Jenny nodded grimly. 'Coates knew all this, of course. No wonder you were all so amused this morning.'

'Yes, Coates knew,' Lewis admitted. 'We all did – but I wasn't laughing. A good rider could get over this track with a bit of luck, but . . . '

' . . . not a girl?' Vicky finished his sentence for him.

'I wouldn't want to ride this race on a half-trained horse. Dancer is a good all-rounder. And your Black Beauty is a very fast runner – if you can get it out of him. But he's hardly broken in, let alone an experienced racer.' Lewis scratched his head. 'If anyone can work miracles with him, though, it might just be you. That horse and you . . . you know each other.'

Lewis paused a moment, then looked at his watch as if he suddenly had to be somewhere else. With a wave of his hand, he was gone, running up the gorge the way he came.

'I think we had better see the rest of this course,' Jenny said. 'You've got your work cut out for you, young lady.'

'I know,' said Vicky. 'But the end is going to be worth it, isn't it, Jenny?'

'If you get there. Think about what Lewis said. Training is important. Beauty is going to have to know your every command, react to your slightest touch. It's not enough that you trust each other. You are going to have to work together as a team.'

In the days that followed, Jenny marvelled at Vicky's dedication to her task. Vicky herself had never realised that she could work as hard for something before – but then, she had never wanted anything as badly before in her life.

No, she thought, that wasn't true. She had wanted her mother to get well again, and she still desperately wished that her father would return home alive. But these things were out of her hands – nothing she could do would change their outcome.

But this race for Beauty was different. She held the key to it in her hands and had resolved to win it no matter what the cost.

'Collect him – ride him straight. Or you'll go right over his head.' Jenny yelled out instructions as Vicky put Beauty through his paces around a makeshift showjumping course in the front field.

Vicky gritted her teeth and did as she was told. Normally, she did not like taking lessons from anyone – she would prefer to stand or fall on her own, and learn from her mistakes. But there was no time for that. So she swallowed her pride and did as she was told.

Jenny pulled out her watch. 'I have a call to make, Vicky.'

Vicky looked worried. 'The race is tomorrow. He's still only half-trained.'

'A little more than that, I think.'

'I'll practice some more while you're out,' Vicky decided.

'No, no,' Jenny urged. 'Go for a ride. Relax . . . you've both earned it. You both need it, too. Why don't you look up some of your old friends? You haven't done that since we arrived.'

'There hasn't really been time.' Going visiting was the very last thing on Vicky's mind.

'Then why don't you go and see Burton about that job again? Whatever happens tomorrow, Vicky, we still have to live here. We still have to settle in this community.' Jenny fixed her with a probing look. 'You really should look up some of your old friends, you know. It will be good for you.'

Vicky nodded. 'I will, I promise . . . after tomorrow.'

'Tomorrow's not the end of the world.'

Vicky looked at her with feeling. 'It will be if I lose.'

Jenny gave her a quick kiss. 'I'm sorry. I wish I could stay, but I have to dash for this appointment.' She hurried back to the horse and trap, gave a light pull on the reins and she was off.

Jenny was right, Vicky thought. A quiet ride was just what Beauty and she needed. She would walk Beauty over the chosen race course so he would know what to expect. Then, on the ride through town, she could stop in on Mr Burton and ask about that job.

They cantered easily from the beach, up the river, searching for the shallow areas that could be most easily crossed. This was the simplest part of the course and, by the time Vicky arrived at Burton's shop, she was feeling hopeful about her chances against Mr Coates.

Mr Burton was inside, up on a ladder, stocking the shelves. He swung around and nearly fell off as Vicky burst in. That girl, he thought grumpily, she always comes at the worst possible time . . . no respect for her elders, that one.

Vicky knew none of this. She just thought Mr Burton was a bit of an old grouch – which, of course, he was. She waited for him to get down from the ladder before asking, 'Mr Burton, have you decided about the job yet?'

Burton's eyes squinted as he racked his brain for some excuse not to give her the job. 'Ah . . . I might need someone slightly older, I think.'

Hilda Burton came in from her blacksmith's workshop as her husband spoke. She caught Vicky's surprised reaction. 'But there are plenty of girls my age delivering mail,' Vicky was saying.

'There are at that,' Hilda chipped in, delighted to see Vicky Denning again.

'It needs someone with a good horse,' Burton said, not wanting to be outdone by two women ganging up on him.

'That's good, because I've got a *very* good horse,' Vicky replied, pointing out of the door to Black Beauty.

Burton sensed victory. 'Aha, yes . . . but will you have him after tomorrow?' he taunted, smiling with a satisfied smack of his lips.

Hilda 'tut-tutted' him, but Vicky thought for a while before answering. 'If I do win, will you give me the job?'

'I'll consider it,' he snapped, turning back to his shelves.

'Why, thank you, Mr Burton,' Vicky said happily, exchanging a triumphant smile with Hilda. To celebrate, Hilda opened the gobstopper jar and took out two large sweets, popping one in Vicky's mouth and the other in her own.

Out of their sight, Mr Burton was fuming. That clever little girl had got him. He didn't like being made to look a fool, especially in front of his wife. Ah . . . well, he thought, there's precious little chance of a girl winning a tough race like that against Frank Coates.

'All right, then,' he said, turning back to face Vicky. 'If you've still got the horse on Monday, you've got the job.'

Vicky's mouth was full to bursting. She couldn't say anything. Burton stared at her. 'Is that agreed?' he demanded.

Vicky nodded vigorously, then ran out of the shop before Burton began to suspect what she had in her mouth. The shopkeeper gazed after her in disgust.

'Girls these days,' he said to Hilda. 'Look at that, not even a word of thanks.'

Beside him, all Hilda could do was nod her head in agreement. Her mouth was full of the luscious gobstopper as well.

From the settlement, it was on to Miller's Gorge – the worst part of the race. Vicky took it very slowly, letting Beauty become familiar with the track. Occasionally, loose rocks would shift under Beauty's hooves. Once or twice the pair almost lost balance completely, but they kept going.

'This will be the last stretch before the final run up the beach, my Beauty,' Vicky told him. 'This will be where it really counts.'

Soon they were back on the beach again. Looking up, Vicky could see some children near the shore-line, digging for shellfish. She smiled in recognition and rode across to meet them. The children squinted up as Vicky leapt from the saddle to say hello.

'Beth . . . Andy . . . remember me?'

The two older children stood up, but remained silent. There was a tense pause, then Vicky turned to the youngest, a girl of about three. 'Hello, Ellen.'

'Hello,' Ellen's tiny voice squeaked.

'I've been meaning to come over and see you, but we've been a bit busy,' Vicky explained. 'We've only just got back, and the place was left in a proper shambles.'

Again, no-one said a word. Then Andrew reached for his bucket of shellfish. 'We've got to get these back to our mother.' The others followed suit, and they ran off leaving Vicky on the beach alone.

'Whatever's the matter?' Vicky yelled out after them. 'Aren't we friends? I thought we were friends.'

Andrew and Beth stopped for a brief moment on the top of a far off sand dune, staring at her as she shouted. Then they dropped out of sight altogether. Vicky felt devastated. Her only friends, she told herself, were back at the farm. And Beauty, of course. Beauty, who she wanted with her everywhere she went . . . for ever.

15

It was the night before the big race, and Vicky's chance encounter with her childhood friends had left her feeling unhappy and rejected.

After dinner, she, Jenny and Manfred sat around the kitchen table, each absorbed in their own thoughts. Jenny was writing up notes from her farm visits and Manfred was re-designing his flying machine, taking up most of the table with his rulers and geometry kit.

Vicky had a book open but she wasn't reading it. Jenny noticed her glum mood. 'Cheer up – there's nothing you can do about the race now until you run it.'

'Until you've won it,' Manfred laughed. 'I know you will, because the good guys always win.'

'It's not that,' Vicky told them. 'I met some of my old friends and they . . . I don't understand it, I'm the same as ever, aren't I?'

'Of course you are,' Jenny said.

'Then why wouldn't they talk to me?'

Jenny thought for a minute. 'Well . . . you dress and talk differently after your time in England. And it *has* been two years.'

That didn't make Vicky feel any better.

'Don't worry,' Jenny continued. 'They'll come round. It will all work out. And whatever happens tomorrow, we won't lose Beauty. Even if we have to muck out Coates' stables for a year.'

'Five years,' Manfred said, keeping in the spirit of things. It made him feel like a part of the family and he was keen to do whatever he could to get Black Beauty back for Vicky.

Jenny laughed. 'Now, it's bedtime, young lady. You get yourself a good night's sleep.'

'Goodnight,' Vicky said to them. It had been a long day and an important one loomed tomorrow. She was going to need all the rest she could get.

After she left, Manfred stood to go. Jenny held out her hand to stop him, then waited before he sat again before she started talking.

'Manfred. I don't know how to say this . . . I'm sorry, but I simply can't afford to employ you after this month. I'll give you references, of course . . .'

Manfred interrupted, as upset as Jenny. 'Please. I would like to stay.'

'Yes I would like you to as well, but . . .'

'I will stay, then, for the bed and food. Yes? Here I can do my work. Soon my flying machine will be ready. And I have other ideas, too.'

'I can't ask you to work for no wages.'

'I am asking you . . .' Manfred replied.

'Don't you ever think about Germany, about home?' Jenny pressed him.

'Here there is power all around – in the wind, in the water. But farmers struggle. They cannot afford to buy stock or machines . . .'

' . . . or wages,' Jenny added with a smile.

'Here I have everything I want. I will find a way to put power into the farmers' hands. At home it's . . . different.'

Jenny considered the serious young man in front of her. She had no doubt he would do what he said. He had a remarkable mind and a gift for being able to create his ideas from the scraps of wood and metal around him. 'I will pay you wages as soon as I am able – agreed?'

'Agreed,' Manfred said readily, shaking her hand. 'And tomorrow, we beat Mr Coates.'

Race day dawned brilliantly fine. Good, Vicky thought, at least the gorge won't be slippery and bogged down in mud.

The three of them – Vicky, Jenny and Manfred – arrived early but there was already a sizeable crowd lined up on the beach.

The idea of such a race had captured the imaginations of people from all over the region. Among them were a fair number of farm labourers – they were betting men, and reckoned Frank Coates would be an easy winner. Most had a few hard-earned shillings riding on him, so they were understandably nervous when they saw Vicky riding on Black Beauty.

Beauty's obvious quality as a race-horse even had some of them thinking about changing their bet.

Then there were the locals, most of whom were backing Vicky. Frank Coates wasn't exactly the most popular man in the district – and there were some who felt it was about time he had his comeuppance.

Vicky surveyed the crowd and saw Beth, Ellen and Andrew among a scatter of kids. She waved to them, but they pretended not to see.

She and Coates rode out to the starting mark. Lewis stood out to one side under the start/finish sign. He took off his hat and held it high above his head.

'Ready?' he asked.

Jenny squeezed Vicky's hand. 'Good luck, my love.'

'Go!' Lewis whipped down his hat. The race had begun.

Coates and Dancer, Vicky and Black Beauty kicked off at the same time. The crowd cheered them on. Soon they were lost from sight of those left behind on the beach.

All that Jenny and Manfred could do was wait anxiously as Vicky and Coates battled it out. They raced neck and neck along the shallow river, then up the winding bridle track that led to town.

By the time they sprinted past Burton's store, Coates had established a slender lead. Hilda watched anxiously for Vicky, her fingers crossed for good luck. As the cloud of dust disappeared, Hilda could see a wagon approaching. Who was this?

A distinguished-looking man with a grey beard stepped down from the wagon. 'Good morning,' he said, in a very British voice. 'Could you please direct me to the Denning farm?'

Hilda passed on the information. Then, as the mysterious man drove off she suddenly realised she had forgotten to ask his name.

Back at the beach, the young men were in a huddle, swapping bets. Bert glanced up at Lewis, who stood a short distance off. He held up four fingers – did Lewis want to bet four shillings on Vicky? Lewis nodded. The odds were three to one – he stood to make twelve shillings if Vicky came through, and he was sure she had a fighting chance.

He looked over at Jenny and gave an encouraging smile, but she was too tense to react. Beside her, Manfred was hopping from one foot to the other, visibly nervous.

'Manfred, stop fidgeting,' Jenny said sharply. 'It doesn't help anyone.'

Coates and Vicky were nearing the gorge. The progress became more difficult and Black Beauty began to fall back. Coates looked behind him and laughed. 'It gets a lot worse than this, missy.'

He leapt ahead. Vicky redoubled her efforts, urging Black Beauty forward. They dashed through the gorge, faster and faster, flying over the timber and rock-strewn ground.

'We're almost there!' Vicky shouted, excited. 'It's almost over, boy.'

But a large log of timber blocked their path. It hadn't been there yesterday. Vicky didn't see it – she took the wrong line and Beauty only just saw it in time. He pulled to a halt but Vicky lost her balance completely and fell forward heavily on to the ground.

In front of them, Coates heard the commotion and stopped. He swung around to see if Vicky was all right. She scrambled to her feet, mudstained and with a slight cut to her cheek, but otherwise unscathed.

'Give up,' Coates demanded. 'It's not worth it.'

'Oh yes it is,' Vicky replied, her voice full of emotion. 'And you know it.'

She jumped back into the saddle and urged Black Beauty forward. Even Coates could not help but be impressed by her pluck. He set off again, stubbornly holding on to his lead.

The crowd was waiting expectantly, straining for first sight of the horses when they emerged on the beach. Manfred shielded his eyes from the harsh sun – he saw some movement in the distance.

'Somebody coming,' he cried.

The people stirred. They could just make out a horse and rider, but who was it?

Lewis recognised them first. 'It's Coates,' he shouted.

'Come on Vicky – come on!' Jenny willed her to appear, but Coates was already surging nearer and there was still no sign of Vicky or Black Beauty.

Finally they appeared. There was a lot of ground to make up, but Beauty looked strong. 'Pay up, Lewis. They haven't got a chance,' Bert sneered.

'I'll pay when I've lost – not before,' Lewis answered. But Bert was right, Vicky's chances did not look good.

'Oh no, oh no, oh no,' Manfred kept repeating. Jenny gave him a sharp look.

'Don't give up on her yet, Manfred. She's still got a chance.'

Vicky studied the gap between her and Coates. She had tried everything, but Coates' experience had her beat. Then she remembered what Lewis and Jenny had said about teamwork, about how the way to run this race was for her and Beauty to run it together.

She leaned forward over Beauty's neck and talked to him. 'Now Beauty, for both of us . . . we *can* do it. Together. Ride, ride, ride . . .'

As if in answer to her prayers, Vicky was rocked by a sudden explosion of energy from Black Beauty. The big black horse seemed to gather reserves of speed from nowhere and sprinted ahead.

Slowly the gap between the two horses started to close, but the finishing line was in sight. It still looked like Coates would be a clear winner.

Beauty's hooves thundered over the firm, smooth sand. The crowd fell silent, awed, as Vicky and Beauty began to draw back the impossible distance at impossible speed.

Lewis was smiling – he knew Beauty had it in him. Bert was counting out the money he now looked certain to lose. Burton, the shopkeeper, stood with his mouth gaped open – in all his years he never would have believed it!

Jenny and Manfred stood quiet and proud as a loud cheer rang out from the crowd. Coates looked around and was stunned to see Vicky flying up to him with every passing stride. Soon, they were racing, neck and neck, then, another surge, and

Beauty flashed past, increasing his lead by one length, then two as they crossed the finishing line.

Jenny and Manfred rushed forward to congratulate her. Vicky half-dismounted and half-collapsed from the saddle into their arms. They embraced as well-wishers crowded around.

'We won! We won!' was all Vicky could say. She threw her arms around Black Beauty's neck in a tearful embrace.

A small hand came up and joined Vicky's. She turned to see Beth, Ellen and Andrew beside her. They didn't seem as suspicious or wary as they had been the day before.

'That was wonderful, Victoria,' Beth said shyly.

'It's Vicky, If you don't mind . . . or I'll start calling you Elizabeth!'

The three children smiled at Vicky's response. So that was it, she thought, they decided I'd turned into a snob after being in England. The children ran off, laughing. That was another problem solved – all in all it had been a very satisfying day.

Just then, Coates came over to see them, leading Dancer. He handed the reins to Vicky. 'Here,' he said gruffly.

Vicky looked puzzled. What was all this about? 'Winner take all, wasn't it,' Coates said, harshly. 'Here you are . . .'

'I've got the horse I want, Mr Coates,' Vicky answered. She and Jenny turned their backs on him, leaving Coates shamefaced,. He had competed for greed, certain that he would win. Now she had beaten him in the race, Vicky also showed herself to be a charitable and unselfish champion.

Coates left the beach, muttering to himself. No-one else wanted to listen. Bert and Lewis were heatedly having their own argument about who owed who how much money.

'Right,' Jenny announced. 'Let's get you home and cleaned up. I think we can forget about chores for you tonight.'

Manfred and Vicky laughed. Then she spied Mr Burton, attempting to scurry away unnoticed. 'Mr Burton,' she called out, 'thanks for the job! I'll start work on Monday.'

With all those people around, there was nothing Mr Burton could do. He smiled – well, it was the nearest he could get to a smile – and he waved, and he hurried off as quickly as he could.

Jenny took hold of Vicky's arm. 'Home,' she said.

They arrived back at the farm without Manfred. 'Poor old thing,' Jenny said. 'He should really learn to ride. Horses don't get flat tyres.'

'And they're friends for life, right, Beauty?' Vicky was elated. All the way home, she couldn't stop hugging her new horse or thinking about what Lewis had said after the race.

'That's a fine beast you've won for yourself,' he had told her. But he was wrong, Vicky thought. We won each other. From now on, we will look after each other the way special friends always do.

They cantered through the open gate and stopped by the front verandah. Vicky and Jenny exchanged glances, but didn't say a word. Piled up by the front door was a stack of luggage. The door was half open.

They crept noiselessly inside and opened the kitchen door. Sitting in a chair, sipping a cup of tea like he owned the place, was Dr Gordon.

'Father!' cried Jenny, her sense of shock quickly giving way to joy. 'What on earth are you doing here?'

Dr Gordon stood up with a beaming smile and embraced his daughter, saving another special hug for Vicky.

'I caught a fast steamer shortly after sending you my last letter . . . '

Jenny blinked the tears from her eyes. 'Well, what if we'd been on our way home? What would you have done then?'

'That's a silly question to ask your father. I know my daughter, and I think I know Vicky. You two, I thought, would just be stubborn enough to stay on and fight it out. Well, you're not going to fight it out without me here with you.'

Vicky grabbed Dr Gordon's hand.

'Come and see Black Beauty!'

After all his travelling, you could have knocked Dr Gordon down with a feather. 'Who?' he replied, startled at the name. He was the one who had buried Black Beauty back in England.

'Come on,' Vicky cried, out the door already.

Jenny and Dr Gordon followed and watched as Vicky put Beauty through some gentle paces.

'Do you recognise the horse?' Jenny asked.

'Oh yes,' Dr Gordon answered. 'And the girl riding it. I know them both very well indeed.'

He put his arms around Jenny. It was uncanny, he thought, how similar this new horse seemed to the old Black Beauty. What an emotional reunion. Any worries he had harboured about coming to New Zealand were gone.

He looked over at Vicky, so like Jenny had been fifteen years ago. She stood Beauty up on his hind legs in a triumphant rear and waved. Dr Gordon closed his eyes, freezing the moment in his mind like a photograph.

They were home.